The Golden Windmill & Other Stories by Stacy Aumonier

Stacy Aumonier was born at Hampstead Road near Regent's Park, London on 31st March 1877.

He came from a family with a strong and sustained tradition in the visual arts; sculptors and painters.

On leaving school it seemed the family tradition would also be his career path. In particular his early talents were that of a landscape painter. He exhibited paintings at the Royal Academy in the early years of the twentieth century.

In 1907 he married the international concert pianist, Gertrude Peppercorn, at West Horsley in Surrey. A year later Aumonier began a career in a second branch of the arts at which he enjoyed a short but outstanding success—as a stage performer writing and performing his own sketches.

The Observer newspaper commented that "...the stage lost in him a real and rare genius, he could walk out alone before any audience, from the simplest to the most sophisticated, and make it laugh or cry at will."

In 1915, Aumonier published a short story 'The Friends' which was well received (and was subsequently voted one of the 15 best stories of 1915 by the Boston Magazine, Transcript).

Despite his age in 1917 at age 40 he was called up for service in World War I. He began as a private in the Army Pay Corps, and then transferred as a draughtsman in the Ministry of National Service.

By now he had four books published—two novels and two books of short stories—and his occupation is recorded with the Army Medical Board as 'author.'

In the mid-1920s, Aumonier received the shattering diagnosis that he had contracted tuberculosis. In the last few years of his life, he would spend long spells in various sanatoria, some better than others.

Shortly before his death, Stacy Aumonier sought treatment in Switzerland, but died of the disease in Clinique La Prairie at Clarens beside Lake Geneva on 21st December 1928. He was 55.

Index of Contents

The Golden Windmill
A Source of Irritation
The Brothers
"Old Iron"
Little White Rock
A Good Action
Them Others
The Bent Tree
The Great Unimpressionable
Stacy Aumonier – A short Biography
Stacy Aumonier – A Concise Bibliography

The Golden Windmill

At the top of the hill the party halted. It had been a long trek up and the sun was hot. Monsieur Roget fanned himself with his hat, and his eye alighted on a large pile of cut fern-leaves.

"But this will suit me admirably!" he remarked, and he plumped his squat little figure down, and taking out his large English pipe he began to stuff tobacco into it.

"My little one," said his stout wife, "I should not advise you to go to sleep. You know that to do so in the afternoon always gives you an indisposition."

"Oh, la la! No, no, no, I do not go to sleep, but—this position suits me admirably!" he replied.

"Oh, papa, papa! ... lazybones!" exclaimed his pretty daughter Louise. "And if we leave you, you will sleep like a dormouse."

"It is very hot!" rejoined the father.

"Leave him alone," said Madame Roget," and we will go down to that place that looks like an inn, and see whether they will sell us milk. Where is Lisette?"

"Lisette! Where should she be?"

And of course it was foolish to ask. Lisette, the younger daughter, had been lost in the wood on the way up, with her fiance, Paul Fasquelle. Indeed, the party had all become rather scattered. It is a peculiarity of picnics. Monsieur Roget's eldest son, Anton, was playing at see-saw with his three children on the trunk of a fallen tree. His wife was talking to Madame Aubert, and occasionally glancing up to exclaim:

"Careful, my darlings!" Monsieur Roget was left alone.

He lighted his pipe, and blinked at the sun. One has to have reached a mature age to appreciate to the full the narcotic seductiveness of good tobacco on the system, when the sun is shining and there is no wind. If there is wind all the pleasant memories and dreams are blown away, but if there is no wind the sun becomes a kind, confidential old fellow. He is very, very mature. And Monsieur Roget was mature. He was fifty-nine years old, given to corpulence, rather moist and hot, but eminently comfortable leaning against the pile of ferns. A glorious view across the woods of Fontainebleau lay stretched before him, the bees droned in the young gorse, his senses tingled with a pleasurable excitement, and, as a man will in such moments, he enjoyed a sudden crystallized epitome of his whole life. His struggles, and failures, and successes. On the whole he had been a successful man. If he died tomorrow, his beloved ones would be left in more than comfort.

Many thousand francs carefully invested, some house-property in the Rue Renoir, the three comestibles establishments all doing reasonably well.

Things had not always been like that. There had been long years of anxiety, worry and even poverty.

He had worked hard and it had been a bitter struggle. When the children were children, that had been the anxious time. It made Monsieur Roget shudder to look back on it. But, God be praised! he had been fortunate, very fortunate in his life-companion. During that anxious time, Madame Roget had been patient, encouraging, incredibly thrifty, competent, resourceful, a loyal wife, a very—Frenchwoman. And they had come through. He was now a proud grandfather. Both his sons were doing well, and were married. Lisette was engaged to a very desirable young advocate. Of Louise there need be no apprehension. In fact, everything ....

"Name of a dog! that's very curious," suddenly thought Monsieur Roget, interrupting his own pleasant reflections.

And for some minutes he could not determine exactly what it was that was curious. He had been idly gazing at the clump of buildings lower down the hill, whither his wife and daughter had gone in search, of milk. Perhaps the perfume. of the young gorse had something to do with it, but as he looked at the buildings," he thought:

"It's very familiar, and it's very unfamiliar. In fact, it's gone wrong. They've been monkeying with that gable on the east side, and they've built a new loft over the stables."

But how should he know? What was the gable to him? or he to the gable? He drew in a large mouthful of smoke, held it for some seconds, and then blew it out in a cloud round his head.

Where was this? When had he been here before? They had driven out to a village called Pavane-en-Bois, and from there they had walked, and walked, and walked. He may have been here before, and have come from another direction ....

"Oo-eh!"

Monsieur Roget was glad that he was alone when he uttered this exclamation, which cannot convey what it is meant to in print. Of course, across there on the other side of the clearing was the low stone wall, and the reliquary with the figure of the Virgin, and doubtless at the bottom of the slope the other side would be the well!

It was exactly on this spot that he had met Diane- God in heaven! how long ago? Ten, twenty, thirty.... Exactly thirty-seven years ago!

And how vividly it could all come back to one! He was twenty-two then, a slim young man—considered elegant and rather distinguished-looking by some people—an orphan, without either brothers or sisters, the inheritor of a quite substantial competence from his father, who had been a ship-broker at Marseilles. He had gone to Paris to educate himself and to prepare for a commercial career. He was a serious young man, with modest ambitions, rather moody and given to abstract speculations. Paris bewildered him, and he used to escape when he could, and seek solitude in the country. At length he decided that he must settle down to some definite career, and he became articled to a firm of chartered accountants: Messrs. Manson et Cie. He took rooms at a quiet pension near the Luxembourg, and there fell in love with his patron's daughter, Lucile, a demure and modest brunette. The affair was almost settled, but not quite. Monsieur Roget, even in those days, was a man who never put his leg over the wall till he had seen the other side. He was circumspect, cautious, and there was indeed plenty of time.

And then one day he had found himself on this identical hillock. He could not quite clearly remember how he came to be there. Probably he had come for the day, to escape the clamor of Paris. He certainly had no luggage. He was seated on is spot, dreaming and enjoying the view, when he heard a cry coming from the other side of the low stone wall. He jumped up and ran to it, and lo! on the other side he beheld—Diane! The name was peculiarly appropriate. She was lying there on her side like a wounded huntress. "When she caught sight of him she called out:

"Ah, monsieur, will you be so kind as to help me? I fear I have sprained my ankle."

Paul Roget leapt the wall and ran to her assistance. (The thought of leaping a wall now made him gasp!) He lifted her up, trembling himself, and making sympathetic little clucks with his tongue. "Pardon, pardon! very distressing!" he murmured, when she stood erect.

"If monsieur will be good enough to allow me to rest my hand on his shoulder, I shall be able to hop back to the auberge."

"With the greatest pleasure. Allow me."

On the ground was an upturned pail. He remarked:

"Would it distress mademoiselle to stand for one minute, whilst I re-fill the pail? II

"Oh, no, no," she exclaimed ... "Do not inconvenience yourself."

"Then perhaps mademoiselle will allow me to return for the pail?"

"Oh, no, if you please! My father will do it."

She leant on his shoulder and hopped a dozen paces. "How did it happen, mademoiselle?

"Imbecile that I am! I think I was dreaming. I had filled the pail and was descending the embankment when I slipped. I tried to step across the pail, but caught my foot in the rim. And then I don't know quite what happened. I fell. It is the other ankle which I fear I have sprained."

"I am indeed most desolated. Is it far to the inn?"

"You see it yonder, monsieur. It is perhaps ten minutes walk, but twenty minutes hop."

She laughed gayly, and Monsieur Roget said solemnly:

"If I might suggest it I think it would be more comfortable for Mademoiselle if she would condescend to place her arm round my neck."

"It is too good of you."

They proceeded another hundred paces in silence, and then rested against a stile. Suddenly she gave him one of her quick glances, and said:

"You are very silent, monsieur."

"I was thinking—how very beautiful the day is. As a matter of fact, he was not thinking anything of the sort. He was in a fever. He was thinking how very beautiful, adorable, attractive this lovely wild creature was hanging round his neck. He had never before adventured such an experience. He had never kissed Lucile. Women were an unopened book to him, and lo! suddenly the most captivating of her sex was clinging to him. He felt the pressure of her soft brown forearm on the back of his neck. Her little teeth were parted with smiles, and she panted gently with the exertion of hopping. Her dark eyes searched his, and appeared to be slightly mocking, amused, interested.

"If only I might pick her up and carry her," he thought, but he did not dare to mate the suggestion.

Once she remarked:

"Oh, but I am tired," and he thought she looked at him slyly.

The journey must have occupied half-an-hour, and she told him a little about herself. She lived with her father. Her mother had died when she was a baby. It was quite a small inn, frequented by charcoal-burners and woodmen, and occasionally by visitors from Paris. She liked the country very much, but sometimes it was dull—oh, dull, dull, dull!

"Ah, it is sometimes dull, even in Paris!" sighed Monsieur Roget.

"You must come and speak to my father, and take a glass of wine," she remarked.

In the forecourt of the inn the father appeared.

"Hullo!" he exclaimed. "What is all this?"

He was a rubicund, heavy-jowled gentleman, who by the wheezy exhalations coming from his chest gave the impression of being a chronic sufferer from asthma. Diane laughed.

"I have been through fire and water, my dear," she said, "and this is my deliverer."

She explained the whole episode to the landlord, who shook hands with Paul, and they led the girl into a sitting-room at the back of the cafe. Paul was somewhat diffident about entering this private apartment, but the landlord wheezed:

"Come in, come in, monsieur."

They sat Diane down on a sofa, and the landlord pulled off her stocking. In doing so he revealed his daughter's leg as far as the knee. She had a very pretty leg, but the ankle was considerably swollen.

"The ankle is sprained," said the landlord.

"Will you allow me to go and fetch a doctor?" asked Paul.

"It is not necessary," replied the landlord." I know all about sprained ankles. When I was in the army I served in the ambulance brigade. We will just bind it up very tight with cold linen bandages. Does it hurt, little one?"

"Not very—yet. It tingles. I feel that it may. Won't you offer Monsieur—I do not know his name—some refreshment? "

"Monsieur Paul Roget," said that gentleman, bowing. "But please do not consider me. The sufferer must be attended first. Later on, I would like to be permitted to partake of a little lunch in the inn."

While the landlord, whose name was Jules Couturier, was binding up his daughter's ankle, Paul slipped out and returned to the well, filled the pail, and brought it back to the yard of the inn. "But this is extremely agreeable of you, monsieur," exclaimed the landlord, as he came bustling through the porch. "She will do well. I know all about sprained ankles. Oh, yes! I have had great experience. I beg you to share a little lunch with us. We are quite simple folk, but I think we may find you an omelette and a ragout. Quite country people, you know; nothing elaborate."

The lunch was excellent, and Diane had the sofa drawn up to the table, and in spite of the pain she must have been suffering, she laughed and joked, and they were quite a merry party. After lunch he helped to wheel her out into the crab apple orchard at the back, and he told her all about himself, his life and work, and ambitions. He told her everything, except perhaps about Lucile. And he felt very strange, elevated, excited.

When the evening came he left it till too late to catch the train back to Paris, and the landlord lent him some things and he stayed the night.

He stayed three nights, and wrote to Messrs. Manson et Cie, and explained that he had gone to Pavane-en-Bois, and had been taken ill. He wrote the same thing to Lucile. And during the day he talked to Diane, and listened to the landlord. Sometimes he would wander into the woods, but he could not bring himself to stay away for long. He brought back armfuls of flowers which he flung across her lap. He touched her hands, and trembled, and at night in bed he choked with a kind of ecstasy and regret. It was horribly distracting. He did not know how to act. He was behaving badly to Lucile, and dishonorably to Manson et Cie. His conscience smote him, but the other little fiend was dancing at the back of his mind. Nothing else seemed to matter. He was mad—madly in love with this little dark-eyed huntress.

At the end of three days he returned to Paris, but not till he had promised to come back at the earliest opportunity.

"Perhaps I will go again in August," he sighed in the train. It was then the seventh of June.
On the fifteenth of June he was back again in the "Moulin d'Or." Diane was already much better.

She could hobble about alone with the help of two sticks. She was more bewitching than ever. He stayed three weeks, till her ankle was quite well, and they could go for walks together in the woods. And he called her Diane, and she called him Paul. And one day, as the sun was setting, he flung his arms round her and gasped:

"Diane ... Diane! I love you!"

And he kissed her on the lips, and her roguish eyes searched his. "Oh, you!" she murmured." You bad boy ... you!"

"But I love you, Diane. I want you. I can't live without you. You must come away with me. We will get married. We will build a world of our own. Oh, you beautiful! Tell me you love me, or I shall go mad!"

She laughed that low, gurgling, silvery laugh of hers.

"What are you saying?" she said. "How should I know? I think you are—a nice boy. But I cannot leave my father."

"My dear, he managed all the time you had to lie with your foot up. Don't torture me! Oh, you must love me, Diane. I couldn't love you so much if you didn't love me a little in return"

"Perhaps I do," she said, smiling.

"What is it, then, Diane?"

"Oh, I don't know. I do not want to marry. I want to be free, to see the world. I am ambitious. I have been to the conservatoire at Souboise. They say I can sing and dance. My father has spent his savings on me."

"Darling, if you marry me, you shall be free. You shall do as you like. You shall dance and sing and see the world. Everything of mine shall be yours if only you will love me. You must-you must. Diane!"

"Well ... we shall see. Come; father will be anxious."

In July he left his pension and moved out to Mont-martre. He had never definitely proposed to Lucile, but his expressions of affection had been so definite that he felt ashamed. He spent his holiday in August at the "Moulin d'Or." And Diane promised to marry him" one day."

"Diane," he said, "I will work for you. You have inspired me. I shall go back to Paris and think of you all day, and dream of you all night."

"That won't give you much time to make your fortune, my little cabbage."

"Do not mock me. Where would you like to live? "

"In Paris, in Nice, in Rome, in Vienna. And then, one day, I would like to creep back here and just live in the 'Moulin d'Or.'"

"The 'Moulin d'Or'?"

"Oh, we could improve it. We could build an extra wing, with a dancing-hall, and more nice bedrooms, and a garage. We could improve the inn, but we could not improve these beautiful hills. Isn't that true, little friend?"

"Nothing could be improved where you are. You are perfection."

"Yes, but—"

In September Diane came to Paris. She stayed with an aunt in Parnasse, and attended a conservatoire of dancing. And every evening Paul called on her, and took her flowers and chocolates and trinkets. And in the daytime, when the image of Diane's face did not interpose between his eyes and his desk, he worked hard. He meant to work hard and become a rich man, and take Diane to Nice, and Rome, and Vienna, and make the structural alterations to the "Moulin d'Or."

In a few months' time Diane made such progress that she was offered an engagement in the ballet at Olympia. She accepted it and Paul was consumed with a fever of apprehension. Every night he went to the performance, waited for her, and escorted her home. But he disliked the atmosphere of the music-hall intensely, and the other girls, Diane's companions—Heaven defend her!

And then she quarreled with her aunt, and Paul besought her to marry him so that he might protect her. But she prevaricated, and in the end he took some rooms for her, and she consented to allow him to pay for them. She lived there for several weeks alone, only attended by an old concierge, and then she took a friend, Babette Baroche, to share the rooms with her, and Paul still continued to pay. Paul disliked Babette. She was a frivolous, vain, empty-headed little cocotte, and no fit companion for Diane. On occasions Paul discovered other men enjoying the hospitality of the rooms, and they were always of an objectionable sort. And Diane got into debt, and he lent her four hundred francs.

At Christmas-time she was dismissed from her engagement, and in a pertinacious mood she promised to marry him in the spring. Paul was delirious. Nothing was good enough for his Diane, and he engaged a complete flat for her, with the services of an elderly home. Diane was very grateful and loving, and in the transition Babette was dropped. However, a, few weeks after he had signed the lease, she was offered an engagement for a tour, and after a lengthy dispute and many tears, she had her way and accepted it. She was away three months, and Paul was consumed with dread, and doubt, and gloomy forebodings. On occasions he dashed down to Lyons, or Grenoble, or wherever she happened to be, for the week-end. And he thought that the company she was with were a very fast lot.

"But, my angel," he would exclaim, "only another month or two, and all this will be over. You will be mine forever and ever."

He was still paying the rent of the flat in Paris, and it was necessary to send Diane flowers and presents wherever she was. It was an expensive time, particularly as, owing to Diane having had her purse stolen just when she was paying off a debt, he had to send her another four hundred francs. She returned at the end of March, and so great had been her success on tour that an egregious, oily manager named Bonnat offered her a part in a new revue. She received a good salary, but the management would not supply her frocks. It was necessary to dress well for this part. It was her first real chance. She ransacked shops in the Rue de Tivoli, and Paul accompanied her.

Eventually she spent twelve hundred francs on them, and Paul advanced the money. She only allowed him to do so on the understanding that she paid him back by installments out of her salary. It is needless to say that she never did so. However, the frocks were a great success, and Diane made a hit. She was undoubtedly talented. She danced beautifully, and she had a gift of imitation. She very quickly became a star, and of course a star could not scintillate in the poky little flat she had so far occupied. She moved to a more fashionable quarter, and occupied a flat the rent of which was rather more than her salary alone. She developed more expensive tastes, and. nearly always kept a taxicab waiting for her at stage-doors and restaurants.

At this time Paul began to realize that he was living considerably above his income. It would be necessary to reduce it by breaking into his capital. He sold some house property and paid Diane's debts and bought her a pearl pendant.

"Next month she will be my wife," he thought, "and then I shall be able more easily to curb these extravagancies."

But when the next month came Diane was at the height of her success. She had been given more to do in the revue, and her imitations were drawing the town. The management raised her salary. Her head was completely turned.

"Oh, no, no, no! dear heart," she exclaimed. "Not this month. At the end of the season. It would be imbecile when I have all Paris at my feet."

Paul begged and urged her to reconsider, but she was obdurate. She continued the same life, only that her tastes became more and more extravagant. And one day Paul took her to task.

"My angel-flower," he said, "we must not go on like this. All the savings for our wedding are vanishing. I am eating into my capital. We shall be ruined."

"But, my little love," replied Diane, "I spend so little. Why, you should see the electric brougham Zenie at the Folies Bergeres has. Besides, next year, or perhaps before, they will have to double my salary."

"Yes, but in the meantime—?"

"In the meantime your little girl shall kiss away your naughty fears."

And of course Diane soon had an electric brougham of her own. The more salary she had, the more it seemed to cost Paul. He was receiving merely a nominal salary himself from Messrs. Manson et Cie, where he was little more than a pupil. However, at that time he managed to get a small increase, and invested a good bulk of his patrimony in a rubber company that a very astute business friend advised him about. If the shares went up considerably he might sell out, and reimburse himself for all these inroads on his capital.

In the meantime a disturbing element crept into his love affair. A depraved young fop, the Marquis de Lavernal, appeared on the scene. He was one of those young men who have plenty of money and frequent stage-doors. He was introduced by Babette, whom he almost immediately forsook for Diane. He called upon her, left more expensive flowers and chocolates than Paul could afford, and one day took her to Long-champs in his car.

Paul was furious.

"This man must not come here," he exclaimed. "I shall kill him!"

"Oo-oh! but why? He is quite a nice boy. He is nothing to me. He is Babette's friend,"

"I don't trust him. I won't have him here. Do you understand, Diane? I love you so, I am distracted when that kind of person speaks to you!"

"Oo-oh!"

Diane promised not to see him again alone, but Paul was dubious. The trouble was that he did not know what went on in the daytime. In the evening he could to a certain extent protect her. But in the daytime—that raven! that ogre! that blood-sucker! He was the kind of man who had the entree of all theaters, both the back and the front. He went about with parties of girls. Diane explained that it was impossible sometimes not to meet him. He was always with her friends.

At the end of July Paul had a stroke of fortune. The rubber shares he had bought went up with a great boom, quite suddenly. He sold out and netted a considerable sum. And then he had a brilliant inspiration. He would tell Diane nothing of this. He had plans of his own.

One day he took the train and went down to see his prospective father-in-law at the "Moulin d'Or." The old man was wheezier than ever, but very cordial and friendly.

"Well, my boy, how goes it?" he asked.

"Excellently," said Paul. "Now, father-in-law, I have a proposition to make. Diane and I are to be married after the summer season. It has always been her ambition to live at the' Moulin d'Or.' But she has spoken of improvements. I want to suggest to you with all respect that you allow me to make those improvements. I would like to do it without her knowing it, and then to bring her down as a great surprise."

"Well, well, very agreeable, I'm sure. And why not? It would be very charming!"

"I suggest building a new wing, with a dancing-hall and several nice bedrooms, and a garage; and laying out the gardens more suitably."

"Well, good! It would be very desirable, and conducive to good business. You may rely upon me to assist you in your project, Monsieur Paul."

"I am indeed grateful to you, Monsieur Couturier."

Paul returned to Paris in high spirits. He made plans of the suggested alterations on the back of an envelope, in the train. The next morning he went to an eminent firm of contractors. So feverish was he in his demands that he persuaded them to send a manager down that very day to take particulars and prepare the estimate. The work was commenced the same week.

In the meantime, Diane had bought some expensive little dogs, because Fleurie at the Odeon kept expensive little dogs, and a new silver tea-service because Lucie Castille at the Moulin Rouge had a silver tea-service. And Paul was surprised because neither of the accounts for these luxuries was sent to him. Diane said she had paid for them herself, but the little demons of jealousy were still gnawing away at his heart.

The revue was to terminate at the end of the third week in August, and Paul said:—

"And then, my love, we will marry quietly in Paris, and then we will do the grand tour. We will go to Nice, and Rome, and Vienna, and commence our eternal honeymoon at the 'Moulin d'Or.'"

Diane clapped her hands.

"Won't that be beautiful, my beloved!" she exclaimed, and she twined her sinuous arms around his neck. "Fancy! just you and I alone at the dear ' Moulin d'Or! Ah! and then we will go to Venice, and to Munich. Good gracious! It will be soon time to think about the frocks and trousseau!"

Paul's heart swelled. The trousseau! Diane was becoming serious. There had been moments when he had doubted whether she meant to marry him at all, but the trousseau! Why, yes, the matter must be attended to at once. They spent three weeks buying Diane's trousseau. Nearly every day she thought of something fresh, some little trifle that was quite indispensable. When the bills came in they amounted to twenty-two thousand francs! Paul was aghast. He had no idea it was possible to spend so much on those flimsy fabrics. And furniture had yet to be purchased. He went to his astute business friend again, and begged for some enticing investment. He was recommended a Nicaraguan Company that was just starting. They had acquired the rights of a new method of refining oil. It was going to be a big thing. With the exception of a sum of money to pay for the improvements at the "Moulin d'Or" Paul put practically the whole of his capital into the Nicaraguan Company. Nearly every day he called at the contractor's, or sent frenzied telegrams to Monsieur Couturier to inquire how the work was progressing. At length he received a verbal promise that the whole thing would be completed by about the twentieth of September.

Excellent! That would fit in admirably. It would give him a month's honeymoon with his beautiful Diane, and then, one glorious September evening, he would drive up the hill, and jumping out of the car in the new drive he would be able to exclaim:

"Behold! Do not all your dreams come true?"

And Diane would fling her arms round his neck, and the old father would come toddling out and find them in that position, and he would probably weep, and it would all be very beautiful.

A few days later there was a rather distressing incident. Quite on her own responsibility Diane ordered a suite of Louis XVI furniture. They were fabulously expensive copies. Paul had nothing like enough money to pay for it. He did not want to sell his Nicaraguan shares. In fact, he had only just applied for them. He protested vehemently:

"But, my dear, you ought not to have done this! It is ruinous. We cannot afford it."

"But, my Carlo, one must sit down!"

"One need not pay fifteen thousand francs to sit down!"

"Oo-oh!"

Paul knew the evidence of approaching tears, and he endeavored to stem the tide. In the end he went to a money-lender and borrowed the money at an abnormal rate of interest, and then he went to Diane and said:

"My beloved, you must promise me not to spend any more money without my consent. The consequences may be serious. My affairs are already getting very involved. You must promise me."

Diane promised, and the next day drove to his office in a great state of excitement. Bonnat had been to see her. They wanted to take the revue for a two months' tour to Brittany and Normandy, commencing at Dinard on August 22nd. He had offered her dazzling terms. She simply must go. It might be her last chance. The wedding must be postponed till the end of October. Paul protested, and they both became angry and cried before two other clerks in Messrs. Manson's office. They parted without anything being settled. When he saw her at night after the theater, she had signed the contract. And Paul returned to his rooms, and bit his pillow with, remorse and grief.

On the twenty-first of August Diane locked up her trousseau, and the furniture, and left with the company for Dinard. And Paul wrote to her every day, and she replied once a week, and occasionally sent him a telegram announcing a prodigious success. Only occasionally did he get an opportunity of going to her over a week-end. The journeys were very long and he resented spending the money. In only one way did he derive any satisfaction from that tour. The building work—like all building work—could not possibly be completed in the time specified. If they had arrived there on the twenty-first of September, his beautiful Diane would have found the place all bricks and mortar and muddle. As it was, it would be comfortably finished by the middle of October.

When not going to Diane he would spend Sunday with Monsieur Couturier, who was keenly excited about the improvement to his inn. It was going to be very good for the business. All the countryside spoke of it. The patron of the "Colonne de Bronze," further down the hill, was furious, and this was naturally a matter of satisfaction to Monsieur Couturier. He was proud of and devoted to his future son-in-law.

At the end of September came the great blow. Paul heard of it first through the newspapers. The Nicaraguan Company had failed. The refining process had proved efficient, but far more expensive to work than any other refining process. The company was wound up, and the shareholders received about 20 per cent. on their investments. Paul was practically ruined. He would have to pay for the building of the "Moulin d'Or." Beyond that he had only a few thousand francs, and he had to meet the promissory note of the moneylenders, he wrote to Diane and confessed the whole story. She sent him a telegram which simply said: Courage! courage!"

He wore the telegram inside his shirt for three days, till it got rather too dilapidated. Then he concentrated on his work. Yes! he would have courage. He would build up again. Diane trusted him.

In any case, they could sell the furniture and go and live at the "Moulin d'Or." He wrote her long letters full of his schemes. On October the twelfth the work was completed, and he went down and spent two days and nights with Monsieur Couturier. Diane was to return to Paris on the fifteenth. Monsieur Couturier was full of sympathy and courage. They talked far into the night of how they would manage. With the increase of business assured, the inn would no doubt support the three of them. There were great possibilities, and Paul was young and energetic. Nothing mattered so long as his Diane believed in him.

The night before he returned to Paris he went for a walk in the woods by himself. He visualized the days to come, the walks with Diane, the tender moments when they held each other's hands; he could see their children toddling hand in hand through the woods, picking flowers. In an ecstasy he rushed to a thick bush, and picked a bunch of red berries. He would take them to Diane.

They would be the symbols of their new life. Wild flowers from their home, not exotic town-bred things. It was all going to be joy ... joy ... joy!

He ran back to the inn, and spent a sleepless night, dreaming of Diane and the days and nights to come.

In the morning came a letter from Messrs. Manson et Cie. His dealings with the money-lenders had been disclosed. His services were no longer desirable.

Well, there it was! It would take more than that to crush him in his ecstatic mood. He would start again. He would begin by helping Monsieur Couturier to run the inn.

He returned to Paris late in the evening. He would go to Diane's flat after she had returned from the theater. She would be a little sleepy, and comfortable, and comforting. She would wear one of those loose, clinging, silky things, and she would take him in her arms, and he would let down her beautiful dark blue-black hair, and then he would make her a coronet of the red berries. He would make her his queen ....

He was too agitated to dine that evening. He walked the streets of Paris, clasping the red berries wrapped in tissue paper. He kept thinking:

"Now she is resting between the acts. Now she is dancing a pas seul in the second act. Now she is giving her imitation of Yvette Guilbert. Now she is taking a call. Now the manager speaks to her, congratulating her—curse him! Now she awaits her cue to go on again."

He was infinitely patient. He restrained his wild impetus to rush to the theater. He hung about the streets. He meant to stage-manage his effect with discretion. He waited some time after the theater was closed. Then, very slowly, he walked in the direction of her flat. As he mounted the stairs, he began to realize that he was very exhausted. He wished that he had not foregone his dinner. However, after the first rapturous meeting with Diane, he would take a glass of wine. Very quietly he slipped the key in the lock, and let himself in. (He had always had a key to Diane's flat, which was in effect his flat.) Directly he had passed the door he heard loud sounds of laughter. He swore inwardly. How aggravating! Diane had brought home some of her friends! There were evidently a good many of them, from the noise and ribaldry. In the passage were several bottles and glasses.

He crept along silently to the portiere concealing the salon. He could hear Diane's voice. She was speaking, and after each sentence the company screamed with laughter. Ah! she was entertaining them with one of her famous imitations. He stood there and listened. He made a tiny crack in the curtain and peeped through. Diane was doing a funny little strut, and speaking in a peculiar way. He listened and watched for three or four minutes before he realized the truth of what he saw and heard. And when he did realize it, he had to exert his utmost will power to prevent himself from fainting.

The person that Diane was imitating was—himself!

The realization seemed to be bludgeoned into him, assisted by a round of ironic cheers. People were calling out:

"Brava! brava! Diane!"

He heard Babette say:

"Where is the little end-of-a-man? "

And Diane's voice reply:

"Oh, he is coming back soon, I believe. I forget when."

A man's voice—he believed it was the Marquis de Lavemal's—exclaimed:

"And when is our Diane going to marry it? "

Diane, very emphatically:

"Do not distress yourself, my dear; he's lost all his money."

A roar of laughter drowned conversation, and Paul groped his way along the passage, still clutching the red berries. He reached the door. Then he reconsidered the matter. He crept back to her bedroom. He placed the berries under the coverlet, and taking a sheet of paper, he wrote one word on it: Good-by."

He placed this on the berries, and then stole out into the night.

Paul was then twenty-two, and his life was finished. He was a crushed and broken man. He wandered the streets of Paris all night. He spent hours grimly watching the encircling waters of the

Seine, the friend and comforter of so many broken hearts. At dawn he returned to his own apartment. He slept for several hours, and then woke up in a fever. He was very ill for some weeks.

But one must not despair forever. At the end of that time, ho pulled himself together, and went out and sought employment. He eventually got a situation as a junior clerk in a wholesale store, and he went back to live at the old pension near the Luxembourg, and he resumed his friendship with Lucile. And in two years' time he married Lucile. And then his life began. His life began. His life began. And lo! here was Lucile walking slowly up the hill, arm-in-arm with her daughter Louise. Yes, his life began ....

"Ah! there you are! What did I say?" exclaimed Louise. He's been asleep!"

"And we've had such an interesting time," added Madame Roget, panting with exertion." We've been to the inn."

"And there's such a pretty girl there," continued the daughter. "You'd fall in love with her, papa."

"Is she very dark?" asked Monsieur Roget.

"Yes, she has blue-black hair and beautiful dark eyes."

"Good God!"

"I knew he would be interested. She gave us some milk, and she has been telling us her story. She's quite young, and she owns the inn, although it's very hard work to run it, she says. She only has one woman and a potman. Her mother was a famous actress, who made a lot of money and bought the inn and improved it. She died when Mademoiselle was fifteen."

"Who was her father? "

"I don't know. I rather gather that her father was a bad lot. He died, too."

"How old is she?"

"Not much more than twenty."

"Then her mother must have been thirty-nine when she died."

"What makes you say so? "

"Of course she must have been. What happened to the old man?"

"What old man?"

"Her grandfather."

"What are you talking about, papa? I don't believe you're quite awake yet."

"She must have had a grandfather. Everybody has a grandfather."

"Well, of course. But—"

"Then he must be either dead or alive."

"How tiresome you are! We must be going. The others are waiting for us lower down the hill." Monsieur Roget struggled to his feet, and shook the little dead fronds of fem from his clothes, and his wife dusted him down behind.

"We shall be going back past the inn," she said.

"The inn! Why can't we go the other way? The way we came?"

"Don't be so absurd. What does it matter? The others are awaiting us."

They went slowly down the hill, and came in sight of the "'Moulin d'Or."

"Isn't it disgusting," remarked Louise, "how these speculative builders are always spoiling the old inns?"

"I don't see it's spoilt," answered her father petulantly.

"You are ridiculous, papa! Any one can see the inn isn't half as nice as it was,"

As they approached the forecourt of the inn, a girl came out carrying a pail. She had dark eyes, blue-black hair, and a swinging carriage. Yes, yes, there was no doubt about it. She was the spit and image of her mother.

As she approached she smiled pleasantly, and said:

"Good evening, mesdames; a pleasant journey. Good evening, monsieur."

The ladies returned a friendly greeting, and Monsieur Roget suddenly turned to the girl and said:

"Is your grandfather alive or dead?" She continued smiling, and replied:

"I do not remember my grandfather, monsieur."

No, perhaps not; it was thirty-seven years ago, and old Couturier was an old man then. Perhaps not.

"Papa, can't you see she's going to the well to fetch water? Why don't you offer to help her?"

"Eh? No, I'm not going. Let her fetch it herself!"

"Papa!"

They walked on in silence till well out of hearing, when Louise exclaimed:

"Really, papa, I can't understand you. So ungallant! It's not like you. You ought to have offered to fetch the water for her, even if she refused."

"Eh? Oh, no! I wasn't going. Very dangerous. You might fall down and sprain your ankle. Oh, no! Or she might fall down, or something. It's very slippery up there by the well. You're not going to get me to do it. Let her fetch her own water. Oh, no! no, no, no, no!"

"Louise dear," remarked Madame Roget. "Let us hurry. Your father is most queer. I always warn him, but it is no good. If he sleeps in the afternoon he always gets an indisposition."

A Source of Irritation

To look at old Sam Gates you would never suspect him of having nerves. His sixty-nine years of close application to the needs of the soil had given him a certain earthy stolidity. To observe him hoeing, or thinning out a broad field of turnips, hardly attracted one's attention, he seemed so much part and parcel of the whole scheme. He blended into the soil like a glorified Swede. Nevertheless, the half-dozen people who claimed his acquaintance knew him to be a man who suffered from little moods of irritability.

And on this glorious morning a little incident annoyed him unreasonably. It concerned his niece Aggie. She was a plump girl with clear, blue eyes, and a face as round and inexpressive as the dumplings for which the county was famous. She came slowly across the long sweep of the downland and, putting down the bundle wrapped in a red handkerchief which contained his breakfast and dinner, she said:

"Well, Uncle, is there any noos?"

Now, this may not appear to the casual reader to be a remark likely to cause irritation, but it affected old Sam Gates as a very silly and unnecessary question. It was, moreover, the constant repetition of it which was beginning to anger him. He met his niece twice a day. In the morning she brought his bundle of food at seven, and when he passed his sister's cottage on the way home to tea at five she was invariably hanging about the gate, and she always said in the same voice:

"Well, Uncle, is there any noos?"

Noos! What noos should there be? For sixty-nine years he had never lived farther than five miles from Halvesham. For nearly sixty of those years he had bent his back above the soil. There were, indeed, historic occasions. Once, for instance, when he had married Annie Hachet. And there was the birth of his daughter. There was also a famous occasion when he had visited London. Once he had been to a flower-show at Market Roughborough. He either went or didn't go to church on Sundays. He had had many interesting chats with Mr. James at the Cowman, and three years ago had sold a pig to Mrs. Way. But he couldn't always have interesting noos of this sort up his sleeve. Didn't the silly zany know that for the last three weeks he had been hoeing and thinning out turnips for Mr. Hodge on this very same field? What noos could there be?

He blinked at his niece, and didn't answer. She undid the parcel and said:

"Mrs. Goping's fowl got out again last night."

"Ah," he replied in a noncommittal manner and began to munch his bread and bacon. His niece picked up the handkerchief and, humming to herself, walked back across the field.

It was a glorious morning, and a white sea mist added to the promise of a hot day. He sat there munching, thinking of nothing in particular, but gradually subsiding into a mood of placid content. He noticed the back of Aggie disappear in the distance. It was a mile to the cottage and a mile and a half to Halvesham. Silly things, girls. They were all alike. One had to make allowances. He dismissed her from his thoughts, and took a long swig of tea out of a bottle. Insects buzzed lazily. He tapped his pocket to assure himself that his pouch of shag was there, and then he continued munching. When he had finished, he lighted his pipe and stretched himself comfortably. He looked along the line of turnips he had thinned and then across the adjoining field of swedes. Silver streaks appeared on the sea below the mist. In some dim way he felt happy in his solitude amidst this sweeping immensity of earth and sea and sky.

And then something else came to irritate him: it was one of "these drafted airyplanes."

"Airyplanes" were his pet aversion. He could find nothing to be said in their favor. Nasty, noisy, disfiguring things that seared the heavens and made the earth dangerous. And every day there seemed to be more and more of them. Of course "this old war" was responsible for a lot of them, he knew. The war was a "plaguy noosance." They were short-handed on the farm, beer and tobacco were dear, and Mrs. Steven's nephew had been and got wounded in the foot.

He turned his attention once more to the turnips; but an "airyplane" has an annoying genius for gripping ones attention. When it appears on the scene, however much we dislike it, it has a way of taking the stage-center. We cannot help constantly looking at it. And so it was with old Sam Gates. He spat on his hands and blinked up at the sky. And suddenly the aeroplane behaved in a very extraordinary manner. It was well over the sea when it seemed to lurch drunkenly and skimmed the water. Then it shot up at a dangerous angle and zigzagged. It started to go farther out, and then turned and made for the land. The engines were making a curious grating noise. It rose once more, and then suddenly dived downward, and came plump down right in the middle of Mr. Hodge's field of swedes.

And then, as if not content with this desecration, it ran along the ground, ripping and tearing twenty-five yards of good swedes, and then came to a stop.

Old Sam Gates was in a terrible state. The aeroplane was more than a hundred yards away, but he waved his arms and called out:

"Hi, you there, you musn't land in they swedes! They're Mister Hodge's."

The instant the aeroplane stopped, a man leaped out and gazed quickly round. He glanced at Sam Gates, and seemed uncertain whether to address him or whether to concentrate his attention on the flying-machine. The latter arrangement appeared to be his ultimate decision. He dived under the engine and became frantically busy. Sam had never seen any one work with such furious energy; but all the same it was not to be tolerated. It was disgraceful. Sam started out across the field, almost hurrying in his indignation. When he appeared within earshot of the aviator he cried out again:

"Hi! you mustn't rest your old airyplane here! You've kicked up all Mr. Hodge's swedes. A noice thing you've done!"

He was within five yards when suddenly the aviator turned and covered him with a revolver! And Speaking in a sharp, staccato voice, he said:

"Old Grandfather, you must sit down. I am very much occupied. If you interfere or attempt to go away, I shoot you. So!"

Sam gazed at the horrid, glittering little barrel and gasped. Well, he never! To be threatened with murder when you're doing your duty in your employer's private property! But, still, perhaps the man was mad. A man must be more or less mad to go up in one of those crazy things. And life was very sweet on that summer morning despite sixty-nine years. He sat down among the swedes.

The aviator was so busy with his cranks and machinery that he hardly deigned to pay him any attention except to keep the revolver handy. He worked feverishly, and Sam sat watching him. At the end of ten minutes he appeared to have solved his troubles with the machine, but he still seemed very scared. He kept on glancing round and out to sea. When his repairs were complete he straightened his back and wiped the perspiration from his brow. He was apparently on the point of springing back into the machine and going off when a sudden mood of facetiousness, caused by relief from the strain he had endured, came to him. He turned to old Sam and smiled, at the same time remarking:

"Well, old Grandfather, and now we shall be all right, isn't it?"

He came close up to Sam, and suddenly started back.

"Gott!" he cried, "Paul Jouperts!"

Bewildered, Sam gazed at him, and the madman started talking to him in some foreign tongue. Sam shook his head.

"You no roight," he remarked, "to come bargin' through they swedes of Mr. Hodge's."

And then the aviator behaved in a most peculiar manner. He came up and examined Sam's face very closely, and gave a sudden tug at his beard and hair, as if to see whether they were real or false.

"What is your name, old man?" he said.

"Sam Gates."

The aviator muttered some words that sounded something like "mare vudish," and then turned to his machine. He appeared to be dazed and in a great state of doubt. He fumbled with some cranks, but kept glancing at old Sam. At last he got into the car and strapped himself in. Then he stopped, and sat there deep in thought. At last he suddenly unstrapped himself and sprang out again and, approaching Sam, said very deliberately:

"Old Grandfather, I shall require you to accompany me."

Sam gasped.

"Eh?" he said. "What be talkie' about? Company? I got these 'ere loines o' turnips—I be already behoind—"

The disgusting little revolver once more flashed before his eyes.

"There must be no discussion," came the voice. "It is necessary that you mount the seat of the car without delay. Otherwise I shoot you like the dog you are. So!"

Old Sam was hale and hearty. He had no desire to die so ignominiously. The pleasant smell of the Norfolk downland was in his nostrils; his foot was on his native heath. He mounted the seat of the car, contenting himself with a mutter:

"Well, that be a noice thing, I must say! Flyin' about the country with all they turnips on'y half thinned!"

He found himself strapped in. The aviator was in a fever of anxiety to get away. The engines made a ghastly splutter and noise. The thing started running along the ground. Suddenly it shot upward, giving the swedes a last contemptuous kick. At twenty minutes to eight that morning old Sam found himself being borne right up above his fields and out to sea! His breath came quickly. He was a little frightened.

"God forgive me!" he murmured.

The thing was so fantastic and sudden that his mind could not grasp it. He only felt in some vague way that he was going to die, and he struggled to attune his mind to the change. He offered up a mild prayer to God, Who, he felt, must be very near, somewhere up in these clouds. Automatically he thought of the vicar at Halvesham, and a certain sense of comfort came to him at the reflection that on the previous day he had taken a "cooking of runner beans" to God's representative in that village. He felt calmer after that, but the horrid machine seemed to go higher and higher. He could not turn in his seat and he could see nothing but sea and sky. Of course the man was mad, mad as a March hare. Of what earthly use could he be to any one? Besides, he had talked pure gibberish, and called him Paul something, when he had already told him that his name was Sam. The thing would fall down into the sea soon, and they would both be drowned. Well, well, he had almost reached three-score years and ten. He was protected by a screen, but it seemed very cold. What on earth would Mr. Hodge say? There was no one left to work the land but a fool of a boy named Billy Whitehead at Dene's Cross. On, on, on they went at a furious pace. His thoughts danced disconnectedly from incidents of his youth, conversations with the vicar, hearty meals in the open, a frock his sister wore on the day of the postman's wedding, the drone of a psalm, the illness of some ewes belonging to Mr. Hodge. Everything seemed to be moving very rapidly, upsetting his sense of time. He felt outraged, and yet at moments there was something entrancing in the wild experience. He seemed to be living at an incredible pace. Perhaps he was really dead and on his way to the kingdom of God. Perhaps this was the way they took people.

After some indefinite period he suddenly caught sight of a long strip of land. Was this a foreign country, or were they returning? He had by this time lost all feeling of fear. He became interested and almost disappointed. The "airyplane" was not such a fool as it looked. It was very wonderful to be right up in the sky like this. His dreams were suddenly disturbed by a fearful noise. He thought the machine was blown to pieces. It dived and ducked through the air, and things were bursting all round it and making an awful din, and then it went up higher and higher. After a while these noises ceased, and he felt the machine gliding downward. They were really right above solid land—trees, fields, streams and white villages. Down, down, down they glided. This was a foreign country. There were straight avenues of poplars and canals. This was not Halvesham. He felt the thing glide gently and bump into a field. Some men ran forward and approached them, and the mad aviator called out to them. They were mostly fat men in gray uniforms, and they all spoke this foreign gibberish. Some one came and unstrapped him. He was very stiff and could hardly move. An exceptionally gross-looking man punched him in the ribs and roared with laughter. They all stood round and laughed at him, while the mad aviator talked to them and kept pointing at him. Then he said:

"Old Grandfather, you must come with me."

He was led to an iron-roofed building and shut in a little room. There were guards outside with fixed bayonets. After a while the mad aviator appeared again, accompanied by two soldiers. He beckoned him to follow. They marched through a quadrangle and entered another building. They went straight into an office where a very important-looking man, covered with medals, sat in an easy-chair. There was a lot of saluting and clicking of heels. The aviator pointed at Sam and said something, and the man with the medals started at sight of him, and then came up and spoke to him in English.

"What is your name? Where do you come from Your age? The name and birthplace of your parents?

He seemed intensely interested, and also pulled his hair and beard to see if they came off. So well and naturally did he and the aviator speak English that after a voluble examination they drew apart, and continued the conversation in that language. And the extraordinary conversation was of this nature:

"It is a most remarkable resemblance," said the man with medals. "Unglaublich! But what do you want me to do with him, Hausemann?"

"The idea came to me suddenly, Excellency," replied the aviator, "and you may consider it worthless. It is just this. The resemblance is so amazing. Paul Jouperts has given us more valuable information than any one at present in our service, and the English know that. There is an award of five thousand francs on his head. Twice they have captured him, and each time he escaped. All the company commanders and their staff have his photograph. He is a serious thorn in their flesh."

"Well?" replied the man with the medals.

The aviator whispered confidentially:

"Suppose, your Excellency, that they found the dead body of Paul Jouperts?"

"Well?" replied the big man.

"My suggestion is this. Tomorrow, as you know, the English are attacking Hill 701, which for tactical reasons we have decided to evacuate. If after the attack they find the dead body of Paul Jouperts in, say, the second lines, they will take no further trouble in the matter. You know their lack of thoroughness. Pardon me, I was two years at Oxford University. And consequently Paul Jouperts will be able to prosecute his labors undisturbed."

The man with the medals twirled his mustache and looked thoughtfully at his colleague.

"Where is Paul at the moment?" he asked.

"He is acting as a gardener at the Convent of St. Eloise, at Mailleton-enhaut, which, as you know, is one hundred meters from the headquarters of the British central army staff."

The man with the medals took two or three rapid turns up and down the room, then he said:

"Your plan is excellent, Hausemann. The only Point of difficulty is that the attack started this morning."

"This morning?" exclaimed the other.

"Yes; the English attacked unexpectedly at dawn. We have already evacuated the first line. We shall evacuate the second line at eleven-fifty. It is now ten-fifteen. There may be just time."

He looked suddenly at old Sam in the way that a butcher might look at a prize heifer at an agricultural show and remarked casually:

"Yes, it is a remarkable resemblance. It seems a pity not to—do something with it."

Then, speaking in German, he added:

"It is worth trying. And if it succeeds, the higher authorities shall hear of your lucky accident and inspiration, Herr Hausemann. Instruct Ober-lieutenant Schultz to send the old fool by two orderlies to the east extremity of Trench 38. Keep him there till the order of evacuation is given, then shoot him, but don't disfigure him, and lay him out face upward."

The aviator saluted and withdrew, accompanied by his victim. Old Sam had not understood the latter part of the conversation, and he did not catch quite all that was said in English; but he felt that somehow things were not becoming too promising, and it was time to assert himself. So he remarked when they got outside:

"Now, look 'ee 'ere, Mister, when am I goin' to get back to my turnips?"

And the aviator replied, with a pleasant smile:

"Do not be disturbed, old Grandfather. You shall get back to the soil quite soon."

In a few moments he found himself in a large gray car, accompanied by four soldiers. The aviator left him. The country was barren and horrible, full of great pits and rents, and he could hear the roar of artillery and the shriek of shells. Overhead, hero planes were buzzing angrily. He seemed to be suddenly transported from the kingdom of God to the pit of darkness. He wondered whether the vicar had enjoyed the runner beans. He could not imaging runner beans growing here; runner beans, aye, or anything else. If this was a foreign country, give him dear old England!

Gr-r-r! bang! Something exploded just at the rear of the car. The soldiers ducked, and one of them pushed him in the stomach and swore.

"An ugly-looking lout," he thought. "If I wor twenty years younger, I'd give him a punch in the eye that 'u'd make him sit up."

The car came to a halt by a broken wall. The party hurried out and dived behind a mound. He was pulled down a kind of shaft, and found himself in a room buried right underground, where three officers were drinking and smoking. The soldiers saluted and handed them a typewritten dispatch. The officers looked at him drunkenly, and one came up and pulled his beard and spat in his face and called him "an old English swine." He then shouted out some instructions to the soldiers, and they led him out into the narrow trench One walked behind him, and occasionally prodded him with the butt-end of a gun. The trenches were half full of water and reeked of gases, powder, and decaying matter. Shells were constantly bursting overhead, and in places the trenches had crumbled and were nearly blocked up. They stumbled on, sometimes falling, sometimes dodging moving masses, and occasionally crawling over the dead bodies of men. At last they reached a deserted-looking trench, and one of the soldiers pushed into the corner of it and growled something, and then disappeared round the angle. Old Sam was exhausted. He leaned panting against the mud wall, expecting every minute to be blown to pieces by one of those infernal things that seemed to be getting more and more insistent. The din went on for nearly twenty minutes, and he was alone in the trench. He fancied he heard a whistle amidst the din. Suddenly one of the soldiers who had accompanied him came stealthily round the corner, and there was a look in his eye old Sam did not like. When he was within five yards the soldier raised his rifle and pointed it at Sam's body. Some instinct impelled the old man at that instant to throw himself forward on his face. As he did so he was aware of a terrible explosion, and he had just time to observe the soldier falling in a heap near him, and then he lost consciousness.

His consciousness appeared to return to him with a snap. He was lying on a plank in a building, and he heard some one say:

"I believe the old boy's English."

He looked round. There were a lot of men lying there, and others in khaki and white overalls were busy among them. He sat up, rubbed his head, and said:

"Hi, Mister, where be I now?"

Some one laughed, and a young man came up and said:

"Well, old man, you were very nearly in hell. Who the devil are you?"

Some one came up, and two of them were discussing him. One of them said:

"He's quite all right. He was only knocked out. Better take him in to the colonel. He may be a spy."

The other came up, touched his shoulder, and remarked:

"Can you walk, Uncle?"

He replied:

"Aye, I can walk all roight."

"That's an old sport!"

The young man took his arm and helped him out of the room into a courtyard. They entered another room, where an elderly, kind-faced officer was seated at a desk. The officer looked up and exclaimed:

"Good God! Bradshaw, do you know who you've got there?"

The younger one said:

"No. Who, sir?"

"It's Paul Jouperts!" exclaimed the colonel.

"Paul Jouperts! Great Scott!"

The older officer addressed himself to Sam. He said:

"Well, we've got you once more, Paul. We shall have to be a little more careful this time."

The young officer said:

"Shall I detail a squad, sir?"

"We can't shoot him without a court-martial," replied the kind-faced senior.

Then Sam interpolated:

"Look 'ee 'ere, sir, I'm fair' sick of all this. My name bean 't Paul. My name's Sam. I was a-thinnin' a loine o' turnips—"

Both officers burst out laughing, and the younger one said:

"Good! damn good! Isn't it amazing, sir, the way they not only learn the language, but even take the trouble to learn a dialect!"

The older man busied himself with some papers.

"Well, Sam," he remarked, "you shall be given a chance to prove your identity. Our methods are less drastic than those of your Boche masters. What part of England are you supposed to come from? Let's see how much you can bluff us with your topographical knowledge."

"I was a-thinnin' a loine o' turnips this mornin' at 'alf-past seven on Mr. Hodge's farm at Halvesham when one o' these 'ere airyplanes come down among the swedes. I tells 'e to get clear o' that, when the feller what gets out o' the car 'e trains a revowlver and 'e says, 'You must 'company I—'"

"Yes, yes," interrupted the senior officer; "that's all very good. Now tell me—where is Halvesham? What is the name of the local vicar? I'm sure you'd know that."

Old Sam rubbed his chin.

"I sits under the Reverend David Pryce, Mister, and a good, God-fearin' man he be. I took him a cookin' o' runner beans on'y yesterday. I works for Mr. Hodge, what owns Greenway Manor and 'as a stud-farm at Newmarket, they say."

"Charles Hodge?" asked the young officer.

"Aye, Charlie Hodge. You write and ask un if he knows old Sam Gates."

The two officers looked at each other, and the older one looked at Sam more closely.

"It's very extraordinary," he remarked.

"Everybody knows Charlie Hodge," added the younger officer.

It was at that moment that a wave of genius swept over old Sam. He put his hand to his head and suddenly jerked out:

"What's more, I can tell 'ee where this yere Paul is. He's actin' a gardener in a convent at—" He puckered up his brows, fumbled with his hat, and then got out, "Mighteno."

The older officer gasped.

"Mailleton-en-haut! Good God! what makes you say that, old man?"

Sam tried to give an account of his experience and the things he had heard said by the German officers; but he was getting tired, and he broke off in the middle to say:

"Ye have n't a bite o' somethin' to eat, I suppose, Mister; or a glass o' beer? I usually 'as my dinner at twelve o'clock."

Both the officers laughed, and the older said:

"Get him some food, Bradshaw, and a bottle of beer from the mess. We'll keep this old man here. He interests me."

While the younger man was doing this, the chief pressed a button and summoned another junior officer.

"Gateshead," he remarked, "ring up the G.H.Q. and instruct them to arrest the gardener in that convent at the top of the hill and then to report."

The officer saluted and went out, and in a few minutes a tray of hot food and a large bottle of beer were brought to the old man, and he was left alone in the corner of the room to negotiate this welcome compensation And in the execution he did himself and his county credit. In the meanwhile the officers were very busy. People were coming and going and examining maps, and telephone bells were ringing furiously. They did not disturb old Sam's gastric operations. He cleaned up the mess tins and finished the last drop of beer. The senior officer found time to offer him a cigaret, but he replied:

"Thank 'ee kindly, sir, but I'd rather smoke my pipe."

The colonel smiled and said:

"Oh, all right; smoke away."

He lighted up, and the fumes of the shag permeated the room. Some one opened another window, and the young officer who had addressed him at first suddenly looked at him and exclaimed:

"Innocent, by God! You couldn't get shag like that anywhere but in Norfolk."

It must have been an hour later when another officer entered and saluted.

"Message from the G.H.Q., sir," he said.

"Well?"

"They have arrested the gardener at the convert of St. Eloise, and they have every reason to believe that he is the notorious Paul Jouperts."

The colonel stood up, and his eyes beamed. He came over to old Sam and shook his hand.

"Mr. Gates," he said, "you are an old brick. You will probably hear more of this. You have probably been the means of delivering something very useful into our hands. Your own honor is vindicated. A loving Government will probably award you five shillings or a Victoria Cross or something of that sort. In the meantime, what can I do for you?"

Old Sam scratched his chin.

"I want to get back 'ome," he said.

"Well, even that might be arranged."

"I want to get back 'ome in toime for tea."

"What time do you have tea?"

"Foive o'clock or thereabouts."

"I see."

A kindly smile came into the eyes of the colonel. He turned to another officer standing by the table and said:

"Raikes, is any one going across this afternoon with dispatches?"

"Yes, sir," replied the other officer. "Commander Jennings is leaving at three o'clock."

"You might ask him if he could see me."

Within ten minutes a young man in a flight-commander's uniform entered.

"Ah, Jennings," said the colonel, "here is a little affair which concerns the honor of the British army. My friend here, Sam Gates, has come over from Halvesham, in Norfolk, in order to give us valuable information. I have promised him that he shall get home to tea at five o'clock. Can you take a passenger?"

The young man threw back his head and laughed.

"Lord!" he exclaimed, "what an old sport! Yes, I expect I can manage it. Where is the God-forsaken place?"

A large ordnance-map of Norfolk (which had been captured from a German officer) was produced, and the young man studied it closely.

At three o'clock precisely old Sam, finding himself something of a hero and quite glad to escape from the embarrassment which this position entailed upon him, once more sped skyward in a "dratted airyplane."

At twenty minutes to five he landed once more among Mr. Hodge's swedes. The breezy young airman shook hands with him and departed inland. Old Sam sat down and surveyed the familiar field of turnips.

"A noice thing, I must say!" he muttered to himself as he looked along the lines of unthinned turnips. He still had twenty minutes, and so he went slowly along and completed a line which he had begun in the morning. He then deliberately packed up his dinner. things and his tools and started out for home.

As he came round the corner of Stillway's meadow and the cottage came in view, his niece stepped out of the copse with a basket on her arm.

"Well, Uncle," she said, "is there any noos?"

It was then that old Sam really lost his temper.

"Noos!" he said. "Noos! Drat the girl! What noos should there be? Sixty-nine year' I live in these 'ere parts, hoein' and weedin' and thinnin', and mindin' Charlie Hodge's sheep. Am I one o' these 'ere storybook folk havin' noos 'appen to me all the time? Ain't it enough, ye silly, dab-faced zany, to earn enough to buy a bite o' some' to eat and a glass o' beer and a place to rest a's head o'night without always wantin' noos, noos, noos! I tell 'ee it 's this that leads 'ee to 'alf the troubles in the world. Devil take the noos!"

And turning his back on her, he went fuming up the hill.

The Brothers

In the twilight of his mind there stirred the dim realization of pain. He could not account for this nor for his lack of desire to thrust the pain back. It was moreover mellowed by the alluring embraces of an enveloping darkness, a darkness which he idly desired to pierce, and yet which soothed him with its caliginous touch. Some subconscious voice, too, kept repeating that it was ridiculous, that he really had control, that the darkness was due to the fact that it was night, and that he was in his own bed. In the room across the passage his mother was sleeping peacefully. And yet the pain, which he could not account for, seemed to press him down and to rack his lower limbs.

There was a soothing interval of utter darkness and forgetfulness, and then the little waves of febrile consciousness began to lap the shores of distant dreams, and visions of half forgotten episodes became clear and pregnant.

He remembered standing by the French window in their own dining-room, his mother's dining-room, rapping his knuckles gently on the panes. Beneath the window was the circular bed of hollyhocks just beginning to flower, and below the terrace the great avenue of elms nodding lazily in the sun.

He could hear the coffee-urn on its brass tripod humming comfortably behind him while he waited for his mother to come down to breakfast. He was alone, and the newspaper in his hand was shaking. War! He could not grasp the significance of the mad news that lay trembling on the sheets. His mother entered the room, and as he hurried across to kiss her he noted the pallor of her cheeks.

They sat down, and she poured him out his coffee as she had done ever since he could remember. Then, fixing her dark eyes on his and toying restlessly with the beads upon her breast, she said:

"It's true, then, Robin?"

He nodded, and his eyes wandered to the disfiguring newspaper. He felt as though he were in some way responsible for the intrusion of the world calamity into the sanctity of his mother's life; he muttered:

"It's a dreadful business, mother."

His gaze wandered again out of the window between the row of elms. Geddes, the steward, was walking briskly, followed by two collies. Beyond the slope was a hay-cart lumbering slowly in the direction of the farm. "Parsons is rather late with the clover," he thought. He felt a desire to look at things in little bits; the large things seemed overpowering, insupportable. Above all, his mother must not suffer. It was dreadful that any one should suffer, but most of all his mother. He must devote himself to protecting her against the waves of foreboding that were already evident on her face. But what could he say? He knew what was uppermost in her mind—Giles! He had no illusions.

He knew that his mother adored his elder brother more passionately than she did himself. It was only natural. He too adored Giles. Everybody did. Giles was his hero, his god. Ever since he could remember, Giles had epitomized to him everything splendid, brave, and chivalrous. He was so glorious to look at, so strong, so manly. The vision of that morning merged into other visions of the sun-lit hours with Giles—his pride when quite a little boy if Giles would play with him; his pride when he saw Giles in flannels, going in to bat at cricket; the terror in his heart when one day he saw Giles thrown from a horse, and then the passionate tears of love and thankfulness when he saw him rise and run laughing after the beast. He remembered that when Giles went away to school his mother found him crying, and told him he must not be sentimental. But he could not help it. He used to visualize the daily life of Giles and write to him long letters which his brother seldom answered. Of course he did not expect Giles to answer; he would have no time. He was one of the most popular boys at school and a champion at every sport.

Then the vision of that morning when the newspaper brought its disturbing news vanished with the memory of his mother standing by his side, her arm round his waist, as they gazed together across a field of nodding com ....

Troubled visions, then, of Giles returning post-haste from Oxford, of himself in the village talking to every one he met about "the dreadful business," speaking to the people on the farm, and to old Joe Walters, the wheelwright, whose voice he could remember saying: "Av, tha' woan't tak' thee, Master Robin." He remembered talking to Mr. Meads at the general shop, and to the Reverend Quirk, whose precious voice he could almost hear declaiming:

"I presume your brother will apply for a commission."

He had wandered then up on to the downs and tried to think about "the dreadful business" in a detached way, but it made him tremble. He listened to the bees droning on the heather, and saw the smoke from the hamlet over by Wodehurst trailing peacefully to the sky. "The dreadful business" seemed incredible.

It was some days later that he met his friend Jerry Lawson wandering up there, with a terrier at his heels. Lawson was a sculptor, a queer chap, whom most people thought a fanatic. Jerry blazed down on him:

"This is hell, Robin. Hell let loose. It could have been avoided. It's a trade war. At the back of it all is business, business, business. And millions of boys will be sacrificed for commercial purposes. Our policy is just as much at fault as—theirs. Look what we did at—"

For an hour he listened to the diatribe of Lawson, tremulously silent. He had nothing to reply. He detested politics and the subtleties of diplomacy. He had left school early owing to an illness which had affected his heart. He had spent his life upon these downs and among his books. He could not adjust the gentle impulses of his being to the violent demands of that foreboding hour. When Lawson had departed, he had sat there a long time. Was Lawson right?

He wandered home, determining that he would read more history, more political economy; he would get to the root of "this dreadful business."

He wanted to talk to Giles, to find out what he really thought, but the radiant god seemed unapproachable; or rode roughshod over the metaphysical doubts of his brother, and laughed. Giles had no misgivings. His conscience was dynamically secure. Besides, there was "the mater."

"When I go, Rob, you must do all you can to buck the mater up." He had looked so splendid when he said that, with his keen, strong face, alert and vibrant, Robin had not had it in his heart to answer. And then had come lonely days, reading news books and occasionally talking with Lawson. When Giles went off to his training he spent more time with his mother, but they did not discuss the dreadful thing which had come into their lives. His mother became restlessly busy, making strange garments, knitting, attending violently to the demands of the household. Sometimes in the evening he would read to her, and they would sit trying to hide from each other the sound of the rain pattering on the leaves outside. He had not dared talk to her of the misgivings in his heart or of his arguments with Lawson ....

And then a vision came of a certain day in October.

The wind was blowing the rain in fitful gusts from the sea. He was in a sullen, perverse mood. Watching his mother's face that morning, a sudden fact concerning her had come home to him. It had aged, aged during those three months, and the gray hair on that distinguished head had turned almost white. He felt within him a surging conflict of opposing forces. The hour of climacteric had arrived. He must see it once and for all clearly and unalterably. He had put on his mackintosh then and gone out into the rain. He walked up to the long wall by Gray's farm, where on a fine day he could see the sea; but not to-day, it was too wet and misty; but he could be conscious of it, and feel its breath beating on his temples.

He stood there, then, for several hours, under the protection of the wall, listening to the wind and to the gulls who went shrieking before it. He could not remember where he had wandered to after that, except that for some time he was leaning on a rock, watching the waves crashing over the point at Youlton Bay. And then in the evening he had written to Lawson.

"I want to see this thing in its biggest, broadest sense, dear Jerry."

He knew he had commenced the letter in this way, for it was a phrase he had repeated to himself at intervals.

"Like you, I hate war and the thought of war. But, good heaven! need I say that? Every one must hate war, I suppose. I agree with you that human life is sacred .... But would it be sacred if it stood still?—if it were stagnant?—if it were just a mass affair? It is only sacred because it is an expression of spiritual evolution. It must change, go on, lead somewhere ....

"Don't you think that we on this island have as great a right to fight for what we represent as any other nation? With all our faults and poses and hypocrisies, haven't we subscribed something to the commonwealth of humanity?—something of honor, and justice, and equity? I don't believe you will deny all this. But even if you did, and even if I agreed with you, I still should not be convinced that it was not right to fight. As I walked up by the chalk-pit near Gueldstone Head, and saw the stone-gray cottages at Lulton nestling in the hollow of the downs, and smelt the dear salt dampness of it all, and felt the lovely tenderness of the evening light, I thought of Giles and what he represents, and of my mother, and what she represents, and of all the people I know and love with all their faults, and I made up my mind that I would fight for it in any case, in the same way that I would fight for a woman I loved, even if I knew she were a harlot .... "

Lying there in his bed, these ebullient thoughts reacted on him. Drowsiness stole over his limbs, and he felt his heart vibrating oddly. There seemed to be a sound of drums, beating a tattoo, of a train rumbling along an embankment. And in fancy he was on his way to London again, with the memory of his mother's eyes as she had said:

"Come back safely, Robin boy."

The memory of that day was terrifying indeed. He was wandering about a vast building near Whitehall, tremulously asking questions, wretchedly conscious that people looked at him and laughed. And then that long queue of waiting men! Some were so dirty, so obscene, and he felt that most of them were sniggering at him. A sergeant spoke sharply, and he shuddered and spilt some ink on one of the many forms he had to fill up. Every one seemed rough and violent. After many hours of waiting he was shown into another room and told to strip. He sat with a row of other men, feeling incredibly naked and very much ashamed. The window was open and his teeth chattered with the cold and the nervous tension of the desperate experience. A doctor spoke kindly to him, and an old major at a table asked him one or two questions. He was dismissed and waited interminably in another room. At last an orderly entered and called his name among some others, and handed him a card. He was rejected.

He returned to Wodehurst that evening shivering and in a mood of melancholy dejection. He was an outcast among his fellows, a being with a great instinct towards expression, but without the power to back it up. The whole thing appeared so utterly unheroic, almost sordid. He wondered about Giles. If presenting oneself at a recruiting office was such a terrifying ordeal, what must the actual life of a soldier be? Of course Giles was different, but—the monotony, the cheerless-ness of barrack life! And then the worse things beyond.

After that he would devour the papers and tramp feverishly on the downs; he tried to obtain work at a munition factory, and was refused; made himself ill sewing bandages and doing chaotic odd jobs. And all the time he thought of Giles, Giles, Giles. What Giles was doing, how Giles was looking, whether he was unhappy, and whether they spoke to him brusquely, like the sergeant had to himself in London.

Then came the vision of the day when Giles came and bade farewell, on his way to France—a terrible day. He could not bring himself to look into his mother's eyes. He felt that if he did so he would be a trespasser peering into the forbidden sanctuary of a holy place. He hovered around her and murmured little banalities about Giles's kit, the train he was to catch, the parcel he was to remember to pick up in London. When it came to parting time, he left those two alone and fled out to the trap that was to take his brother to the station. He had waited there till Giles came, running and laughing and waving his hand. He drove with him to the station, and dared not look back to see his mother standing by the window. They were silent till the trap had passed a mile beyond the village; then Giles had laughed, and talked, and rallied him on his gloomy face.

"I'll soon be back, old man. Buck the mater up, won't you? Whoa, Tommy, what are you shying at? ... By jove! won't it be grand on the sea to-night!"

Oh, Giles! Giles! was there ever any one so splendid, so radiant, so uncrushable? His heart, went out to his brother at that moment, and he could not answer.

So closely were his own sympathies interwoven with the feelings of his brother that he hardly noticed the moment of actual separation on the platform. His heart was with Giles all the way up to London, then in the train again, and upon the sea with him that night.

In his imagination, quickened by a close study of all the literature he could get hold of on the actual conditions out there, he followed his brother through every phase of his new life. He was with him at the base, in rest camps, and in dug outs, and more especially was he with him in those zig-zagging trenches smelling of dampness and decay. On dark nights he would hear the scuttle of rats dashing through the wet holes. He would hear the shriek of shells, and the tearing and ripping of the earth.

He would start up and try to make his way through the slime of a battered trench which always seemed to be crumbling, crumbling. In his nostrils would hang the penetrating smell of gases that had the quality of imparting terror. So vivid were his impressions of these things that he could not detach his own suffering from that of his brother. There were times when he became convinced that either he or Giles was a chimera. One of them did not exist.

He seemed to stand for an eternity peering through a slit in a mud wall and gazing at another mud wall, and feeling the penetrating ooze of dying vegetation creeping into his body. Above his head would loom dark poles and barbarous entanglements. It was as though everything had vanished from the world but symbols of fear and cruelty, which rioted insanely against the heavens, as though everything that man had ever learnt had been forgotten and destroyed; and he growled there in the wet earth, flaunting the feral passions of his remote ancestry. And the cold!—the cold was terrible. . . . He remembered a strange thing happening at that time. During some vague respite from the recurring horror of these imaginings, he had, he believed, been walking out through the meadows, when a numbness seemed to creep over his lower limbs. He could not get back. He had lain helpless in a field when George Carter, one of the farm hands, had found him and helped him home. He had been very ill then, and his mother had sent for Doctor Ewing. He could not remember exactly what the doctor said or what treatment he prescribed, or how long he had lain there in a semi-conscious state, but he vividly remembered hearing the doctor say one day: "It's very curious, madam. I was, as you know, out at the Front for some time with the Red Cross, and this boy has a fever quite peculiar to the men at the front. Has he been out standing in the wet mud?" He could not remember what his mother answered. He wanted to say: "No, no, it's not I. It's Giles," but he had not the strength, and afterwards wondered whether it were an illusion.

He knew that many weeks went by, and still they would not let him walk. That was his greatest trouble, for walking helped him. When he could walk, he could sometimes live in a happier world of make-believe, but in bed the epic tragedy unfolded itself in every livid detail, intensely real.

Long periods of time went by, and still he was not allowed to leave his room. His mother would come and sit with him and read him Giles's letters. They were wonderful letters, full of amusing stories of "rags" and tales of splendid feeds obtained under difficult circumstances. Of the conditions that existed so vividly in Robin's mind there was not one word. To read Giles's letters one would imagine that he was away on a holiday with a party of young undergraduates, having the time of their lives. But the letters had no reality to him. He knew. He had seen it all.

Time became an unrecognizable factor. Faces came and went. His mother was always there, and there appeared another kind face whom he believed to be a nurse; and sometimes Jerry Lawson would come and sit by the bed, and talk to him about the beauties of the quattrocento and other things he had forgotten, things which belonged to a dead world ....

Lying there in bed, he could not detach these impressions very clearly, nor determine how long ago they had taken place. There appeared to be an unaccountable shifting of the folds of darkness, a slipping away of vital purposes, and a necessity for focusing upon some immediate development. This necessity seemed, somehow, emphasized by the overpowering pain that had begun to rack his limbs, more especially his right foot. He wanted to call out, but some voice told him that it would be useless. The night was too impenetrable and heavy, his voice would only die away against its inky pall. There was besides a certain soothing tenderness about it, as though it were caressing him and telling him that he must wait in patience, and all would be well. He knew now that he was sleeping in the open, and that would account for the chilling coldness. At the same time it was not exactly the open. There were walls about and jagged profiles, but apparently no roof or distances. The ground was hard like concrete. He must be infinitely patient and pray for the dawn .... He began to feel the dawn before he saw it. It came like the caressing sigh of a woman as she wakes and thinks of her lover in some foreign clime. Somewhere at hand a bird was twittering, aware too of the coming miracle. Almost imperceptibly things began to form themselves. He was certainly behind a wall, but there was a door, with the upper part leaning in. A phrase occurred to his mind: "The white arm of dawn is creeping over the door." A lovely passage! He had read it in some Irish book. The angle at the top of the door was like a bent elbow. It was very, very like the white arm—of some Irish queen, perhaps, or of the Mother of men—a white arm creeping over the door, and in its whiteness delicately touching the eyelids of the sleeping inmates, whilst a voice in a soft cadence whispered: "Awake! pull back the door, and let me show you the silver splendors of the unborn day."

A heavy dew was falling, and the cold seemed bitter, whilst all around he became aware of the slow unfolding of desolation; except for the leaning door, nothing seemed to take a recognizable shape, everything was jagged and violent in its form and exuded the cloying odors of death.

Somewhere faintly he thought he heard the sound of a comet, bizarre and fantastic, and having no connection with the utter stillness of this place of sorrow.

His eye searched the broken darkness in fugitive pursuit of a solution of the formless void. Quite near him, apparently, was an oblong board which amidst this wilderness of destruction seemed to have escaped untouched. As the dim violet light began to reveal certain definite concrete things, he became aware that on the board were some Roman letters. He looked at them for some time unseeingly. The word written there stamped itself without meaning on his brain. The word was:"

FILLES." He repeated it to himself over and over again. The earth seemed to rock again with a sullen, vibrating passion, as though irritated that the work of destruction was not entirely complete. Things already destroyed seemed to be subjected to further transmutation of formlessness. But still the board remained intact, and he fixed his eyes on it. It imbued him with a strange sense of tranquillity. Filles! A little word, but it became to him a link to cosmic things. The desire to reason passed, as the ability to suffer passed. Across the mists of time he seemed to hear the laughter of children. He could almost see them pass. There were Jeannette and Marie, with long black pigtails and check frocks, and just behind them, struggling with a heavy satchel, little fair-haired Babette. How they laughed, those children! and yet he could not determine whether their laughter came from the years that had passed or from the years that were to come.

But wherever the laughter came from, it seemed the only thing the powers of darkness could not destroy. He lay then for a long time, conscious of a peace greater than any he could have conceived.

And the white arm of dawn crept over the door.

The crowd who habitually came down by the afternoon train trickled out of the station and vanished. The master of Wodehurst came limping through the doorway. His face was bronzed and perhaps a little thinner, but his eyes laughed, and his voice rang out to the steward waiting in the dog-cart:

"Hullo! Sam, how are you?"

He was leaning on two sticks, and a porter followed with his trunks. "Can I help you up, sir?"

"No, it's all right, old man; I can manage."

He pulled himself up and laughed because he hit his knee upon the mudguard.

"It's good to be home, Sam."

"Yes; I expect your mother will be glad, sir," answered Geddes, touching up the horse. "And so will we all, I'm thinking."

They clattered down the road, and the high spirits of the wounded warrior rose. He asked a thousand questions, and insisted on taking the reins before they had gone far. It was dusk when they began to draw near Wodehurst; a sudden silence had fallen on Giles. The steward realized the reason. He coughed uncomfortably. They were passing within a hundred yards of Wodehurst Church. Suddenly he said in his deep burr:

"We were all very sorry, sir, about Master Robin." The eyes of the soldier softened; he murmured: "Poor old chap!"

"I feel I ought to tell you, sir. It was a very queer thing. But one day that young Mr. Lawson—you know, the sculptor—about a week after it all happened, he must have got up at daybreak, I should say—nobody saw him do it. He must have gone down there to the churchyard with his tools, and what do you think? He carved something on the stone—on Mr. Robin's stone."

Giles said quickly: "Carved! What?"

"He carved just under the name and date, 'He died for England.'"

"'He died for England!' He carved that on Robin's grave? What did he mean?"

"I don't know, sir."

"Really! What a rum chap he must be!"

"We didn't know what to do about it, sir. I saw it, and I didn't like to tell your mother, and nobody likes to interfere with a tombstone, it seems profane-like. So there it is to this day.''

"Thank you, Sam. I'll think about it."

"Have you had much pain with your foot, sir?"

Giles laughed, and flicked the horse.

"Oh, nothing to write home about, Sam. I had a touch of fever, you know. I didn't tell the mater. It was later on that I got this smash of my right foot. It happened at—I've forgotten the name; some damned little village on the Flemish border. I was lucky in a way, the shrapnel missed me. It was falling stonework that biffed up my foot. There was a building, a sort of school, I should think. It got blown to smithereens. It was rather a nasty mess-up. I was there for seven hours before they found me—Hullo! I see the mater standing at the gate."

The horse nearly bolted with the violence of Giles's waving arms ....

The dinner—all the dishes that Giles specially loved—was finished. With his arm round his mother's waist and a cigar in the corner of his mouth, he led her into the warm comfort of the white-paneled drawing-room.

"You won't mind my smoking in here to-night, mater?"

"My dear boy!"

They sat in silence, watching the red glow of the log fire. Suddenly Giles said: "I say, mater, do you know an awfully rum thing Geddes told me?"

His mother looked up.

"I think perhaps I know. Do you mean in the—cemetery?" Giles nodded, puffing at his cigar in little nervous inhalations. "Yes. I knew. I saw it, of course. I've sat and wondered."

"Such a rum thing to do! What do you think we ought to do about it, mater?"

He saw his mother lean forward; the waves of silver hair seemed to enshrine the beautiful lines of her drawn face; her voice came whispering:

"Hadn't we better leave it, Giles? ... Perhaps he really did die for England?" The young man glanced at her quickly. He saw her aged and broken by the war. He thought of his brother .... Then he caught sight of his own face in the mirror, lean, youthful, vigorous. The old tag flashed through his mind: "They also serve who only stand and wait. "

He thrust away that emotional expression, and in the manner of his kind stayed silent, rigid, with his back to the fire. And suddenly he said:

"I say, mater, won't you play me something? Chopin, or one of those Russian Johnnies you play so rippingly?"

"Old Iron"

You know how the story goes, of course. Husband and wife just about to retire to bed. Wife yawns, husband knocks out his pipe on the grate and remarks:

"Well, better turn in, I suppose."

Wife replies:

"Yes"; then adds languidly:

"I meant to call round to ask the Cartwrights to dinner on Thursday."

Husband, after prolonged pause:

"I'll pop round and ask them now, if you like. They never go to bed till very late,"

"I wish you would, dear."

Husband pulls on a cloth cap and goes out. Wife yawns again, and picks up The Ladies' Boudoir, and idly examines charmeuse gown, and notes the prices of gloves at Foxtrot's & Fieldfern's. Yawns again more audibly. Collects sewing and places it in work-basket. Takes the kitten out and locks it up in the scullery. Yawns, and walks languidly upstairs. Turns on the light and spends fifteen minutes examining face at various angles in the glass. Begins to disrobe. Thinks sleepily: "Tom's a long time." Brushes out her hair and admires it considerably. Conceives a new way of dressing it for future festivities. Disrobes farther.

Yawns. Disrobes completely and re-robes—dressing- gown. "It's too bad being all this time!"

Vitality slightly stirred in the direction of resentment and a kind of mild apprehension. Lies on the bed and drowsily reviews the experiences of the day. Dreams ... Suddenly starts with a consciousness of cold. Gropes for her wrist-watch. A quarter past one! Jumps from the bed, feeling the cold hand of fear on her heart. Runs downstairs and stares helplessly out of the front door. Pauses to consider a thousand possible eventualities. Returns to bedroom and completely re-robes, not forgetting to do her hair neatly and powder her nose. Puts on cloak and goes out. Cartwrights' house all in darkness. Bangs on the front door and rings bell. Head of old Mr. Cartwright at first-floor window:

"Who the devil's that?"

"It's me. Where's Tom? "

"Tom! Haven't seen him for weeks!"

"Good God! Let me in."

Cartwright family aroused. Panic. Painting scene in drawing-room. Brandy, smelling-salts and eau-de-cologne. Young George Cartwright mounts his bicycle—rides to the police-station; on the way talks to policeman on point duty. No, no one heard anything of a thin man with a snuff-colored mustache. At police-station, no accidents so far reported. Chief inspector will make a note and await developments. Night passes, and the following day. No news.

"Weeks, months, years elapse. Eight years slide easily by. The wife survives her grief. She marries the local organist, a blond and commendable young man. They continue to live in the wife's house. Children gather round her knee. One, two, three, twins, an interval, six, seven handsome blond children. They grow up.

Twenty-two years elapse. They are sitting at tea. The father, the mother and the oldest son, a handsome young man in a gray flannel suit. He kisses his mother and says:

"I must go now, mother dear. I have to take a Bible-class."

He goes out (presumably to the Bible-class). The mother smiles with pride, the father glows with benignity and helps himself to another buttered muffin. Everything perfect. Suddenly the door opens, and an old man in a long gray beard and perambulating manner wanders into the room. He stares at the wife, and mumbles:

"Did you say Thursday or Friday? ... My memory is not what it was ...." And the wife stares at the old man, and then at the blond organist. And the blond organist stares at the mother of his beautiful children, and then at the bearded interloper. And they all stare at each other and feel very embarrassed.

The story is familiar to you? Well, perhaps so. It is the story of the eternal triangle, the most useful pattern of geometrical forms in the construction of a romantic pattern.

Heigho! the trouble with human triangles is that they are never equilateral. Two sides together are invariably greater than the third side.

Jim Canning was the third side of a triangle, and he got flattened out. In fact, his wife used to flatten him out on every possible occasion. She was bigger than he, and she was aided by the tertium quid, Ted Woollams, who was nothing more or less than a professional pugilist. What was Jim to do? In every well-conducted epic the hero performs physical feats which leave you breathless. He is always tall and strong, and a bit too quick with the rapier for any villain who crosses his path. But what about a hero who is small and elderly, of poor physique, short-sighted, asthmatical, with corns which impede his gait? You may say that he has no place in the heroic arena. He should clear out, go and get on with his job, and leave heroism to people who know how to manage the stuff. And yet there was something heroic in the heart of Jim Canning: a quick sympathy, and an instinct for self-sacrifice.

He used to keep a second-hand furniture shop, which, you must understand, is a very different thing from an antique shop. Jim's furniture had no determinate character such as that which is associated with the name of Chippendale, Sheraton or Heppelwhite. It was just "furniture." Well-worn sofas, broken chairs and tables, mattresses with the stuffing exuding from holes, rusty brass beds with the knobs missing, broken pots and mirrors and dumb-bells; even clothes, and screws, false teeth and bird-cages, and ancient umbrellas. But his specialty was old iron. Trays and trays and baskets filled with, scraps of old iron.

His establishment used to be known in Camden Town at that time as "The Muck Shop." At odd times of the day you might observe his small pathetic figure trundling a barrow laden with the spoils of some hard-pressed inhabitant. "What a tale the little shop seemed to tell! Struggle and poverty, homes broken up, drink, ugly passions, desperate sacrifices—a battered array of the symbols of distress. And, somehow, in his person these stories seemed to be embodied. One felt that he was sorry for the people whose property he bought. He was always known as a fair dealer. He paid a fair price and never took advantage of ignorance.

His marriage was a failure from the very first. She was a big, strapping woman, the daughter of a local greengrocer. Twelve years younger than Jim, vain, frivolous, empty-headed and quarrelsome. Her reasons for marrying him were obscure. Probably she had arrived at the time when she wanted to marry, and Jim was regarded as a successful shop-keeper who could keep her in luxury. He was blinded by her physical attractions, and tried his utmost to believe that his wife was everything to be desired. Disillusionment came within the first month of their married life, at the moment, indeed, when Clara realized that her husband's business was not so thriving as she had been led to believe. She immediately accused him of deceiving her. Then she began to sulk and neglect him. She despised his manner of conducting business—his conscientiousness and sense of fair-dealing.

"If you'd put some ginger into it," she once remarked, "and not always be thinking about the feelings of the tripe you buy from, we might have a house in the Camden Road and a couple of servants."

This had never been Jim's ambition. Many years ago he had attended a sale at Shorwell Green, on the borders of Sussex, a glorious spot near the downs, amidst lime-trees and little running streams. It had been the dream of his life that one day he would retire there, with the woman he loved—and her children. When he put the matter to Clara, she laughed him to scorn.

"Not half!" she said." Catch me living among butterflies and blinking cows. The Camden Road is my game."

Jim sighed, and went on trundling his barrow. Well, there it was! If the woman he had married desired it, he must do what she wanted. In any case it was necessary to begin to save. But with Clara he found it exceedingly difficult to begin to save. She idled her day away, bought trinkets, neglected her domestic offices, went to the pictures, and sucked sweets. Any attempt to point out to her the folly of her ways only led to bitter recriminations, tears and savage displays of temper, even physical violence to her husband. Then there came a day when Jim fondly believed that the conditions of their married life would be ameliorated. A child was born, a girl, and they called her Annie. Annie became the apple of his eye. He would hurry back from the shop to attend at Annie's bath. He would creep in at night and kiss the warm skin of her little skull. He would think of her as he pottered around amidst his broken chairs and tables, and utter little croons of anticipatory pleasure. Annie! She would grow up and be the mainstay of his life. He would work and struggle for her. Her life should be a path of roses and happiness. His wife, too, appeared to improve upon the advent of Annie. For a time the baby absorbed her. She displayed a kind of wild animal joy in its existence. She nursed it and fondled it, and did not seem to resent the curtailment of her pleasures. It was an additional mouth to feed; nevertheless their expenses did not seem to greatly increase, owing probably to Clara's modified way of living.

Four years of comparative happiness followed. Jim began to save. Oh! very slowly; very, very slowly. He still had less than three hundred pounds put on one side for—that vague future of settled security. But still it was a solid beginning. In another ten or fifteen years he would still be—well, not quite an old man; an active man, he hoped. If he could save only one hundred pounds a year!

It was at this point that Ted Woollams appeared on the scene. He was the son of a manager of a Swimming Bath. On Sundays he used to box in "Fairyland" for purses of various amounts—he was a redoubtable middle-weight. During the week he swaggered about Camden Town in new check suits, his fingers glittering with rings. He met Clara one evening at a public dance. The mutual attraction appears to have been instantaneous. They danced together the whole evening, and he saw her home.

And then began the squeezing out of the third side of the triangle. Jim was not strong enough for them. At first he professed to see nothing in the friendship. He described Ted as "a jolly young fellow, a great pal of my wife's." And Ted treated him with a certain amount of respect. He called in at odd times, stayed to meals, drank Jim's beer, and smoked Jim's tobacco. The triangle was quite intact. It was Annie who caused the first disruption. She disliked the prize-fighter, and screamed at the sight of him. This led to reprisals when he had gone, and Jim's championship of the child did not help to cement the always doubtful nature of the affection between husband and wife. There were cross words and tears, and once she pushed him over a chair, and, in the fall, cut his temple.

A few days later, Ted Woollams called in a great state of agitation. He wished to see Jim alone. It appeared that a wonderful opportunity had occurred to him. It was a complicated story about a quantity of bonded brandy which he had a chance of acquiring and selling at an enormous profit. He wanted to borrow fifty pounds till Saturday week, when he would pay Jim back sixty. Jim said he would lend him the fifty, but he didn't want any interest.

When Saturday week came, Ted said the deal had fallen through, but he would let him have the money back the following Saturday. In the meantime, he came to supper nearly every night. Sometimes he drank too much beer.

Then Clara began to dress for the part. She bought expensive frocks, and had the account sent in to Jim. She neglected the child.

The months drifted by, and Ted was always going to pay, but he became more and more part and parcel of the household. Jim's savings began to dwindle. He protested to both his wife and Ted, but they treated him with indifference. The boxer began to abuse his familiarity. He would frequently tell Jim that he was not wanted in the drawing-room after supper. When spoken to about the money he laughed and said:

"Oh, you've got plenty, old 'un. Lend us another fiver."

On one occasion Jim was foolish enough to lend him another ten pounds, under the spell of some heartrending story about a poor woman in the street where Woollams lived. This lopsided triangle held together for nearly four years. Jim was unhappy and distracted. He did not know how to act. He could not leave his wife, for the sake of the child. If he turned her out—and he had no legal power to do so—she would probably take Annie with her. And the child was devoted to him. They were great friends, and it was only this friendship which prevented him indulging in some mad act. Several times he ordered Woollams out of the house and forbade him to come again, but the boxer laughed at him and called him an old fool. He knew that his wife was practically keeping the man. They went to cinemas together, and often disappeared for the whole day, but she always returned at night, although it was sometimes two or three in the morning before she did so. Jim had no proof of actual unfaithfulness. Neither could he afford to hire detectives, a course of action which in any case appeared to him distasteful. Far from saving a hundred pounds a year, he was spending more than his income. His savings had dwindled to barely forty pounds. His business was stagnant, but still he trundled his barrow hither and thither, calling out, "Old iron! old iron!" and he struggled to pay the fair price.

During a great period of his life Jim had enjoyed an unaccountable but staunch friendship with a gentleman named Isaac Rubens. Isaac Rubens was a Jew in a slightly similar way of business to himself, and he conducted a thriving house at the corner of the Holy Angel Road. Isaac was in many respects a very remarkable man. Large, florid, and puffy, with keen eagle eyes and an enormous nose, he was a man of profound knowledge of the history and value of objects d'art.

He was moreover a man of his word. He was never known to give or accept a written contract, and never known to break a verbal one. The friendship between these two was in many respects singular. Isaac was a keen man of business, and Jim was of very little use to him. Isaac's furniture was the real thing, with names and pedigrees. He did not deal in old iron but in stones and jewels and ornaments. Nevertheless he seemed to find in Jim's society a certain pleasure. Jim would call on his rounds and, leaving his barrow out in the road, would spend half-an-hour or so chatting with the Jew across the counter.

Sometimes after supper they would call on each other and smoke a pipe and discuss the vagaries of their calling, or the more abstract problems of life and death.

When this trouble came upon Jim he immediately repaired to his friend's house and told him the whole story.

"Oh, dear! oh, dear! This is a bad business! a bad business!" exclaimed Isaac, when it was over. His moist eyes glowed amidst the general humidity of his face. "How can I advise you? An erring wife is the curse of God. You cannot turn her away without knowledge. Thank God, my Lena .... But there! among my people such lapses are rare. You have no evidence of unfaithfulness?"

"No."

"You must be gentle with her, gentle but firm. Point out the error of her ways."

"I am always doing that, Isaac."

"She may get over it—a passing infatuation. Such things happen."

"If it wasn't for the child!"

"Yes, yes, I understand. Oh, dear! oh, dear! very distressing, my friend. If I can be of any assistance-"

He thrust out his large hands helplessly. It is the kind of trouble in which no man can help another, and each knew it. Jim hovered by the door.

"It's nice to have some one to—talk to, anyway," he muttered; then he picked up his cap and shuffled away, calling out:

"Old iron! Old iron!"

Annie was nine when the climax came. An intelligent, pretty child, with dark hair and quick, impulsive manners. Her passionate preference for her father did not tend to smooth the troubles of the household. She attended the grammar school and had many girl-friends. She saw very little of her mother.

One evening Jim returned home late. He had been on a visit to his friend, Isaac. He found Annie seated on the bottom stair, in her nightdress. Her face was very pale and set, her eyes bright. She had been crying. When she saw her father she gasped:

"Daddy! ... Oh, Daddy!"

He seized her in his arms and whispered:

"What is it, my dear? "

Then she cried quietly while he held her. He did not attempt to hurry her. At last she got her voice under control and gasped quietly:

"I had gone to bed. I don't know why it was. I got restless in bed. I came down again softly. I peeped into the sitting-room .... Oh, Daddy!"

"What? What, my love? "

"That man .... That man and—"

"Your mother? "

"Yes."

"He was—"

"He was kissing her and—Oh!"

Jim clutched his child and pressed her head against his breast.

"I went in, ... He struck me."

"What!"

"He struck me because I wouldn't promise not to tell."

"He struck you, eh? He struck you! That man struck you, eh?"

"Yes, Daddy."

"Where is he?"

"They're—up there now. I'm frightened."

"Go to bed, my love. Go to bed."

He carried her up the stairs and fondled her, and put her into bed.

"It's all right, my love. Go to sleep. Pleasant dreams. It's all right. Daddy will look after you."

Then he went downstairs.

A shout of laughter greeted him through the door of the sitting-room. He gripped the handle and walked deliberately in. Ted Woollams was stretching himself luxuriously on the sofa. His heavy sensual face appeared puffy and a little mussed. Clara was lying back in an easy chair, smoking a cigarette. Jim did not speak. He walked up to Ted and without any preliminary explanation struck him full on the nose with his clenched fist. For a moment the boxer appeared more surprised than anything. His eyes narrowed, then the pain of the blow appeared to sting him. He rose from the sofa with a growl. As he advanced upon Jim, the latter thought:

"He's going to kill me. What a fool I was not to strike him with a poker!"

He thrust out his arms in an ineffectual defense. There was something horribly ugly, ugly and revolting in the animal-like lurch of the man bearing down on him ... the demon of an inevitable doom. Jim struck wildly at the other's arms, at the same time thinking:

"My little girl! I promised to look after her."

A jarring blow above the heart staggered him, and as he began to crumple forward he had a quick vision of the more destroying fate, the something which came crashing to his jaw. He heard his wife scream; then darkness enveloped him.

A long and very confused period followed. His glimpses of consciousness were intermittent and accompanied by pain. He heard people talking, and they appeared strangers to him. There was a lot of talking going on, quarreling, perhaps. When he was once more a complete master of his brain he realized abruptly that he was in the ward of a hospital. His jaw was strapped up tight and was giving him great pain; a nurse was feeding him through a silver tube. Two of his teeth were missing. He wanted to talk to her, but found he could not speak. Then he recalled the incident of his calamity. Well, there it was. He had been brought up in a hard school. Old iron!

The instinct of self-preservation prompted him to bide his time. Doubtless his jaw was broken; a long job, but he would get well again. At the end of the journey Annie awaited him. What was the child doing now? Who was looking after her? He passed through periods of mental anguish and misgiving, and then long periods of drowsy immobility. Night succeeded day. To his surprise, on the following afternoon, his wife appeared. She came and sat by the bed, and said:

"Going on all right?"

He nodded. She looked uneasily round, then whispered:

"You needn't have taken on like that. Ted's going off to America, tomorrow fulfilling engagements." Jim stared at the ceiling, then closed his eyes. Ted no longer interested him. He wanted Annie, and he could not ask for her. Clara stayed a few moments, chatted with the nurse, and vanished. Why had she come? Later on, he was removed to the operating theater, and they re-set his jaw. The shift of time again became uncertain. A long while later he remembered a kindly-faced man in a white overall saying;

"Well, old chap, who struck you this blow? "

He bent his ear down to Jim's lips, and the latter managed to reply:

"A stranger."

Isaac came, humid and concerned, and pressed his hand.

"Well, well, I've found you, old friend! A neighbor told me. Distressing indeed. They say you must not talk. Well, what can I do? "

Jim indicated with his hands that he wished to write something down. Isaac produced an envelope and a pencil, and he wrote:

"Go and see my little gal Annie. Send her to me. Keep an eye on her."

Isaac nodded gravely, and went away.

There appeared an eternity of time before the child came, but when she did all his dark forebodings vanished. She came smiling up the ward, and kissed him. They held each other's hands for a long time before she spoke.

"They would not tell me where you were. It was old Mr. Rubens. Oh, Daddy, are you getting better?"

Yes, he was getting better. Much better. During the last two minutes he had improved enormously. He felt that he could speak. He managed to mumble:

"How are you, my love? "

"All right. Mother has been very cross. That horrid man has gone away. Mr. Rubens said you hurt your face. How did it happen, Daddy? "

"I slipped on the stairs, my dear, and fell."

Annie's eyes opened very wide, but she did not speak. He knew by her manner that she did not believe him. At the back of her eyes there still lurked something of that horror which haunted them on the night when she had discovered "that horrid man" embracing her mother. It was the same night that her father "slipped on the stairs." The child was too astute to dissociate the two incidents, but she did not want to distress him.

"I shall come every day," she announced.

He smiled gratefully, and she stayed and chatted with him until the sister proclaimed that visitors were to depart.

From that day the convalescence of Jim Canning, although slow, was assured. Apart from the broken jaw he had suffered a slight concussion owing to striking the back of his head against the wall when he fell. The hospital authorities could not get out of him how the accident happened. Annie and Isaac Rubens were regular visitors, but during the seven weeks he remained in hospital Clara only visited him twice, and that was to arrange about money. On the day that he was discharged he had drawn his last five pounds from the bank.

"Never mind, never mind," he thought to himself; "we'll soon get that back." And within a few days he was again trundling his barrow along the streets, calling out in his rather high tremolo voice, "Old iron! Old iron!"

There followed after that a long period in the life of the Canning family which is usually designated as "humdrum." With the departure of Ted Woollams, Clara settled down into a listless prosecution of her domestic routine. She seldom spoke to her husband except to nag him, or to grumble about their reduced circumstances, and these for a time were in a very serious state. Debts had accumulated, and various odds and ends in the house had disappeared while he had been in hospital. Clara was still smartly dressed, but Annie's clothes, particularly her boots, were in a deplorable condition. But Jim set to work, leaving home in the morning at seven o'clock and often not returning till eight or nine at night. For months the financial position remained precarious. A period of hunger, and ill-temper, and sudden ugly brawls. But gradually he began again to get it under control. Clara had not lost her taste for good living, but she was kept in check by the lack of means. She was furtive, sullen, and resentful. Jim insisted that whatever they had to go without, Annie was to continue with her schooling.

They never spoke of Ted Woollams, but Jim knew that he had only gone away for four or five months. Jim struggled on through the winter months, out in all weathers in his thin. and battered coat. Sometimes twinges of rheumatism distorted his face, but he mentioned it to no one, not even Isaac.

It was in April that a sudden and dramatic change came into Jim's life. One morning he was alone in the shop. It was raining, and no customers had been in for several hours. Jim was struggling with the un-solvable problem of getting things straight and sorted out. Beneath a bed he came across a jumble of indescribable things, bits of iron and broken pots, odd boots, sections of brackets, nameless odd-shaped remnants covered with dust and grime. He sighed. He remembered this lot quite well. They had been a great disappointment to him. He had trundled his barrow all the way down to a sale in Greenwich, where he had been given the tip that there were some good things going. Owing to losing his way, he had arrived late, and all the plums had been devoured by rival dealers. He had picked up this lot at the end of the sale for a few shillings, not that they appealed to him as a good bargain, but because he did not want to feel that he had completely wasted his day. He had brought them back and dumped them under the bed, intending to go through them later on. That was many months ago, long before he had been to the hospital, and there they had remained ever since.

Jim's ideas of dusting were always a little perfunctory. With a small feather brush he flicked clouds of dust from one object to another, Xo; there was nothing here of any value, though that piece of torn embroidery might fetch five shillings, and the small oblong iron box which some one had painted inside and out a dark green might be worth a little more. He picked it up and examined it. A ridiculous notion to paint iron; but there! people were fools, particularly customers. Of course it might be copper or brass. In that case it would be worth more. He pulled out a long jack-knife and scraped the surface. The paint was old but incredibly thick. It must have had a dozen coats or so. When he eventually got down to the surface he found a dark-blue color.

"Um!" thought Jim. "That's a funny thing."

And he scraped a little more, and found some brown and white.

"That's enamel" he said out loud. "An enamel box. Um! I'll show that to Isaac. An enamel box might be worth several pounds."

He put the box on one side, and continued tidying up. That evening, after supper, he wrapped the box up in a piece of newspaper and took it round to his friend.

Isaac adjusted his thickest glasses and examined the spot where Jim had scratched. Then he went to the door and called out:

"Lizzie, bring me some turpentine."

When the turpentine was brought, Isaac began to work away at the surface with a rag and penknife. His face was very red, but he made no remark except once to mutter:

"This paint alone is twenty or thirty years old."

It took him nearly half-an-hour to reveal a complete corner of the box. Then he sat back and examined it through a microscope. Jim waited patiently. At last Isaac put it down and tapped the table.

"This," he said deliberately, "is a Limoges enamel box of the finest period. An amazing find! Where did you obtain it?"

"I bought it at a sale of the effects of an old lady named Brandt, at Greenwich. She died intestate, and had no relatives."

"You are in luck's way, Jim Canning."

"But why was it painted dark-green?"

There are many mysteries in our profession. It was probably stolen many years ago—possibly a century ago. The thief knew that the piece was too well known to attempt to dispose of for some time. So for security he painted it in order to hide it. Then something happened. He may have died or been sent to prison. The box passed into other hands. Nobody worried about it. It was just an old iron box. It has probably been lying in a lumber-room for years."

"It's been lying in my shop for five months. Is it worth a great deal, Isaac?"

Isaac thoughtfully stroked his chin.

"I am of opinion that if it is undamaged, and if the rest of it is up to the standard of this part we have disclosed, it is worth many thousand pounds."

Jim looked aghast.

"But I only gave six-and-sixpence for the lot!"

"It is the fortune of our profession."

The upshot of it was that Jim left the box in Isaac's hands to deal with as he thought fit. At first Isaac wished to waive the question of commission, but when Jim pointed out that but for Isaac's superior knowledge he would probably have sold it for a five-pound note, the Jew agreed to sell it on a ten per cent, basis. Fair bargaining on both sides.

Jim returned home, almost dazed by the news. Was it fair to obtain such a large sum of money in such a way? He had done nothing to deserve it. And yet—who should have it, if not he? The old lady had not even any relations. She was an eccentric who lived alone with a crowd of cats. An enamel box has no attraction to a cat.

He said nothing about his find to his wife or to Annie. He did not wish to buoy them up with false hopes. Perhaps, after all, Isaac might be mistaken, or he may have over-valued the object. A thousand pounds! A dazzling sum. Why, he could almost retire upon it to—Shorwell Green, where it was so quiet and peaceful. But no! Clara would not agree to that—the Camden Road! He detested the Camden Road, but still, there it was. Clara was his wife. It was only fair to consider her wishes, although they were so unhappy together. In any case, it would be a great relief; security for years to come.

He went back to his work as though nothing had happened. Weeks went by, and Jim heard nothing about the enamel box; and then, one morning, he received a note from Isaac asking him to call round at once.

When he entered his friend's shop he knew that something exceptional had happened. Isaac was excited. He glowed and smiled, and was almost jocular.

"Come into my little room," he said.

When they were seated, he elaborately produced a cheque from his vest pocket, and handed it across the table to Jim.

"Here is your little share. I have kept my commission."

It was a cheque for £4,140. Isaac had sold it for £4,600 to a well-known collector.

The rest of that day was like a dream to Jim.

Truly, he returned and pretended to be busy. In the afternoon, he even went out and trundled his barrow, calling out, "Old iron! Old iron!" but he did it more by force of habit.

"I need not do this any more," he kept on thinking. His mind was occupied with many visions. It was a bright spring day, with light fleecy clouds scudding above the chimney-pots. How beautiful it would be in that Sussex vale! The flowers would be out, and the young pollard-willows reflected in the cool streams. Pleasant to lie on the bank and fish, and forget this grimy life. And Annie, racing hither and thither, picking the buttercups and marguerites, and nestling by his side. He could do all this! Freedom, by one of those queer twists of fate.

The day wore on, and he still continued his work in a dazed, preoccupied manner. When the evening came, a feeling of exhaustion crept over him. Yes, probably he was tired. He wanted a rest and change. How fortunate he was. And yet he dreaded breaking the news to Clara. She would immediately demand a complete social upheaval. A new house, new furniture, luxuries, and parties, and social excitements. He arrived home late. During supper he was very silent.

"I will tell her afterwards," he thought. Annie was in bed. She should be told to-morrow. But tonight it must be broken to Clara. After all, it was true, she was his wife. It was the fair thing to do. He tried to recall the moments of passion and tenderness of the early days of their honeymoon, but all the other ugly visions kept dancing before his eyes. He lighted his pipe and gazed around the untidy room. Perhaps she would improve. Perhaps the changed conditions would soften her, and make her more amenable. But still, she was his wife, and if she wished to live in the Camden Road, well ...

It was nearly dark, and Clara went out of the room, humming. She seemed peculiarly cheerful to-night. Almost as if she knew.... He fingered the cheque in his breast-pocket. She had gone upstairs—probably to fetch a novel. She adored a certain kind of novel. "When she came down, he would lay the cheque on the table, and say:

"Look, Clara; see what has happened to us!"

And then he would be a little tender with her, try and make her understand how he felt. They would start all over again.

And then happened a variant of that hypothetical case described at the beginning of this story. Only, in this case it was the woman who went out.

Jim was sitting there with his fingers on the cheque that was to be their means of reconciliation, and with the tears already banked in his unuttered speech, when Clara put her head in the door. She had her hat on. She said:

"I'm going to the post."

Jim removed his hand from his breast-pocket. He sat back, and heard the door slam.

"I'll tell her when she comes in."

But Clara never came in. He waited half-an-hour, and then he thought: "She's gone to some dissipation with a friend. Oh, well, I must wait up till she returns, I suppose. I'm sorry she has disappointed me on—a night like this, though."

He sat dreaming in the chair, till he became suddenly painfully aware of cold. It was quite dark. He lighted the gas. It was one o'clock. He felt his heart beating with a physical dread. Something had happened to Clara. Perhaps she had been run over, at the very moment when everything was going to change for the better for her. He blundered his way out into the hall, where a gas-jet flickered feebly, and groped for his overcoat. On it he found a note pinned. He turned up the gas higher, and read:

"I'm going off to Ted Woollams, I'm sick of you, and the stinking little house. Ted's made a bit in America, and I give you the address. You can do what you like about it, but it's no good you ever trying to get me back.

"Clara."

It was characteristic of Jim Canning that this note made him cry. He was so sensitive to its utter callousness and ingratitude. Then he dabbed his eyes with his old rod handkerchief, and went upstairs. He tapped on Annie's door, then he opened it and said quietly:

"Annie, it's all right, my dear. It's only me. May I come in?"

The sleeping child was awake abruptly. She held out her arms.

"I ought not to have woken you up, my love, only I felt a little—lonely. Annie, would you like to come away with me to a beautiful place in the country, where it's all woods and flowers, and little streams?"

"Oh, Daddy, yes! And would there be lambs, too, and little black pigs, and brown calves?"

"Yes, my dear; all those things; and birds, too, and quietness, and freedom."

"But, Daddy, could we?"

"Yes, dear; I've had some good fortune."

Annie was very wide awake now, and she sat up and clapped her hands. "Oh, Daddy, when can we go? "

"Quite soon, my dear. Perhaps in a few weeks."

When he had closed the door, he dabbed his eyes again, and thought:

"It was unthinking of me. I oughtn't to have woken her up, but—she is all I have."

A week later he wrote to Clara:

"Dear Clara,
"I understand that for the last week you have been living with Ted Woollams. I do not criticize your action. We are all as God made us. I shall in the dew course take diverse proceedings not as an act of hostility to you but that you may marry the man of your choice and be respectable. I also shall share with you the result of a good deal last week in older that you may not want and so close with check for £2020. I think this fair.

"Jim."

It was Isaac who helped him over all the difficult problems which occurred at that time, and it was Isaac who persuaded him that he was overdoing the "fairness" to Clara. He said that under the circumstances he had no moral obligation to Clara, and that £500 would be lavish. So in the end Jim altered the cheque to that amount. It was Isaac who took over the little shop, which he used as a kind of dumping-ground of his superfluous stock. And it was Isaac who, a year after, returned letters addressed to Jim in a handwriting he recognized, "Gone away. Address not known." And it was he who in later years bore the brunt of the wild invective of a drunken harridan who said that her husband had deserted her, and would not hand her any of the fortune he must have inherited. He shook his head sadly, and replied that he knew nothing. Mr. Canning and his daughter had left London. He thought they had gone to Australia.

When she had gone, he said to himself: "It would distress Jim to know that a woman who had once been his wife had sunk to such a condition." As he passed through to the room at the back he smiled and thought:

"How fortunate she did not come in here!" On the table was a large bowl of red and white roses, with the label and card still lying on the table. On the card was inscribed," With love to Uncle Isaac. A"

The postmark on the label was a village in Sussex.

Little White Rock

When their careers are finished, the painter, the author, the architect, the sculptor, may point to this or that, and say, "Lo, this is my handiwork. Future generations shall rejoice in me."

But to the actor and the executive musician there is nothing left but—memories.

Their permanence lies in the memories of the people who loved them. They cannot pass it on. Some one may say to you, "Ah, my boy, you should have heard Jean de Reszke," or,"You should have seen Macready play that part." And you are bound in all politeness to accept this verdict, but if you have not heard Jean de Reszke, nor seen Macready, it leaves no definite impression on you at all. Indeed, the actor is in worse case than the musician. For at the present time there are ingenious mechanical devices for caging the performance of a musician with varying degrees of success, but no mechanism could ever imprison the electric thrill of Joseph Jefferson or Henry Irving on their great nights of triumph. They are gone forever, cast away among the limbo of the myths.

These melancholy reflections occurred to me on the first occasion when I visited Colin Brancker. I met the old chap first of all in the public library. He had a fine, distinguished head, with long, snow-white hair. He was slim, and in spite of a pronounced stoop, he carried himself with a certain distinction and alertness. I was a fairly regular visitor to the library, and I always found him devouring the magazines and newspapers which I particularly wanted to read myself. A misunderstanding about a copy of the Saturday Review led to a few formal expressions of courtesy, on the following day to a casual nod, later on to a few words about the weather; then to a profound bow on his part and an inquiry after his health from me. Once we happened to be going out at the same time, and I walked to the end of the road with him.

He interested me at once. His clear, precise diction, with its warm timbre of restrained emotion, was very arresting. His sympathy about the merest trifles stirred you to the depths. If he said, "What a glorious day it is to-day!" it was not merely a conventional expression, but a kind of paean of all the joy and ecstasy of spring life, sunshine and young lambs frisking in the green meadows.

If he said, "Oh! I'm so sorry," in reply to your announcement that you had lost your 'bus ticket coming along and had had to pay twice, the whole dread incident appeared to you envisaged through a mist of tears. The grief of Agamemnon weeping over the infidelity of Clytemnestra seemed but a trite affair in comparison.

One day, with infinite tact, he invited me to his "humble abode." He occupied the upper part of a small house in Talbot Road. He lived alone, but was apparently tended by a gaunt, middle-aged woman who glided about the place in felt slippers.

The rooms were, as he expressed it, "humble," but not by any means poverty stricken. He had several pieces of old furniture and bric-a-brac, innumerable mementoes and photographs. It was then that I realized the peculiar position of the actor. If he had been a painter I could have looked at some of his work and have "placed" him; but what could you do with an old actor who lived so much in the past? The position seemed to me pitiable.

Doubtless in his day he had been a fine and distinguished actor, and here was I, who knew nothing about him, and did not like to ask what parts he had played because I felt that I ought to know.

Neither was he very informing. Not that he was diffident in speech—he talked well and volubly—but I had to gather what he had done by his various implications. There was a signed photograph of himself in the character of Malvolio, and in many other Shakespearean parts. There were also signed photographs of J. L. Toole and Henry Irving, and innumerable actors, some of whom were famous and others whose names were unfamiliar to me. By slow degrees I patched together some of the romantic tissues of his life. Whatever position he may have held in the theatrical world, he certainly still had the faculty of moving one person profoundly—myself. Everything in that little room seemed to vibrate with romance. One of Irving's photographs was inscribed "To my dear old friend, Colin Brancker." On the circular table was an enamel snuffbox given him by Nellie Farren.

When he spoke of his mother his voice sounded like some distant organ with the vox humana stop pulled out. I gathered that his mother had been a famous French actress. On the piano was a fan given her by the Empress Eugenie. He never spoke of his father. Nearly everything had some intimate association.

I formed a habit of calling on old Brancker on Thursday evenings, when my wife usually visited an invalid aunt. The experience was always a complete entertainment. He knew nothing of my world and I knew nothing of his. I came completely under the spell of his imagery. I had only to touch some trinket on the mantelpiece to set the whole machinery of retrospection on the move. He came haltingly to his subject as though he were feeling for it through the lavender—scented contents of some old drawer. But when the subject was discovered, he brought the whole picture vividly before my mind. I could see those people strutting before the footlights, hear them laugh and joke in their stuffy lodgings and their green-rooms, follow their hard life upon the road, their struggles, and adversities, and successes, and above all the moving throb of their passions and romances.

And then the picture would die out. It had no beginning and no end. It was just an impression. The angle of vision would alter. Something else would appear upon the scene.

After a time, touched with pity for this lonely and derelict old actor, my wife and I occasionally sent him little presents of game and port wine, when such things came our way. I would like to explain, at this point, that my wife is younger than I. Her outlook is less critical and introspective. To use her own expression, she is out to have a good time. She enjoys dances and theaters and gay parties.

And, after all, why shouldn't she? She is young and beautiful and full of life. Her hair—but I digress! In spite of the pheasants and the port, she had never met old Brancker. But one day we all happened to meet at the corner of the Talbot Bead.

I then enjoyed an entirely novel vision of my hero. He was magnificent. The bow he made, the long sweep of the hat, would have put d'Artagnan to shame. When I introduced them, he held her hand for a moment, and said:

"It is indeed a great pleasure."

It doesn't sound very much in print, but Alice completely went under. She blushed with pleasure, and told me afterwards that she thought he was "a perfect old dear." The affair lapsed for several weeks. I still continued to call upon him, and we nearly exhausted the whole gamut of his belongings. We even routed through old drawers where faded remnants of ancient fustian would recall some moving episode of the past. I became greedy for these visionary adventures.

One night, rather late, I found the little white frock. So familiar had I become with my old friend that I was allowed to poke about his room on my own, and ask him questions. It was a'. child's frock, and it lay neatly folded on the top of a chest in the passage. I brought it into the room, where he was sipping his rum-and-water, and said:

"What's this, Mr. Brancker?"

He fixed his eyes upon the frock, and instantly I was aware that he was strangely moved. At first an expression of surprise and bewilderment crept over his face; then I observed a look of utter dejection and remorse. He did not speak, and rather confusedly I went up to him and touched him on the shoulder.

"I'm sorry," I said. "Doubtless there is some story.... I ought not to have ... "Instantly he patted my arm in return, and muttered:

"No, no. It's all right, old boy. I will tell you. Only, not to-night. No, not tonight."

He stood up and took one or two turns up and down the room in silence. I did not dare to intrude into the secret chamber of his memories. Suddenly he turned to me, and putting his arm round my shoulder, he exclaimed:

"Old boy, come in to-morrow. Come to dinner. Bring the wife. Yes, you must both come. Come to dinner at seven-thirty. And then—I will tell you the story of that little white frock."

It happened that a dance my wife had intended going to the following night had fallen through. To my surprise, she jumped at Mr. Brancker's invitation. She said that she thought it would be extremely interesting. I felt a little nervous at taking her. An invitation to dinner for the first time is always a doubtful number.

The social equation varies so alarmingly and unexpectedly. My wife frequently dined at what she called "smart" houses. How could old Brancker possibly manage a dinner in his poky rooms? I warned her to wear her oldest and shabbiest, and to have a sandwich before we started. Needless to say, my advice was ignored. She appeared in a wonderful gown of pearl-gray.

Experience told me it was useless to protest, and I jogged along the street by her side in my tweed suit. And then I had my second surprise. Old Brancker was in immaculate evening dress.

Cunningly-modulated lights revealed a table glittering with silver and glass. I mumbled some apology for my negligence, but in his most courtly way he expressed his pleasure that I had treated him with such friendly lack of ceremony. Nevertheless this question of dress—as so often happens—exercised a very definite effect upon my whole evening. I felt a little out of it. My wife and old Brancker seemed to belong to one world and I to another. Moreover, their conversation flowed easily and naturally. The old actor was in his most brilliant mood, and Alice sparkled and gurgled in response. Although she was younger and Brancker older than I, I felt at times that I was the oldest of the three, and that they were just children playing an absorbing game. And the dinner was the third surprise.

The gaunt woman served it, gliding in and out of the room with a quiet assurance. It was no lodging-house dinner, but the artful succession of little dishes which symbolizes the established creed of superior-living creatures. Wine, too, flowed from long-necked bottles, and coffee was served in diminutive cups. At length, Mrs. Windsor collected the last vestiges of this remarkable feast, but left on the table a silver tray on which were set four liqueur glasses and a decanter of green Chartreuse.

"Let us all sit round the fire," said our host. "But, first, let me press you to have a little of this excellent beverage. It was given me by a holy brother, a man who led a varied life, but who, alas! died in disgrace."

He passed his hand across his brow as though the memory were too sacred to be discussed. I sighed involuntarily, and my wife said brightly:

"Not for me, Mr, Brancker; but you help yourself. And now you're going to tell us the story of the white frock."

He raised his fine head and looked at her. Then he stretched out his long arm across the table and gently pressed her hand.

"I beg of you, dear lady," he said gently, "just one drop in memory of my friend."

The implied sanctity of the appeal could not be denied. Both my wife and I partook of half a glass, and though I am by nature an abstainer, I must acknowledge that it tasted very good. Old Brancker's hand trembled as he poured out the Chartreuse. He drank his at a gulp, and as though the emotion were not yet stilled, he had another one. Then he rose, and, taking my wife's arm, he led her to the easy chair by the fire. I was rather proud of my intimate knowledge of the old actor's possessions, and I pointed out the snuff-box which Nellie Farren had given him, and the photograph of Irving, with its inscription "To my dear old friend."

Brancker sighed and shrugged his shoulders. Perhaps one does not boast of these associations. Perhaps it is vulgar, but I knew how interested Alice would be. When we had done a round of the rooms, whither in his fatherly way he had conducted my wife by the arm, and occasionally rested his hand ever so lightly on her shoulder, we returned to the dining-room, and Alice said:

"Now show me this little white frock!"

He bowed, and without a word went out into the hall, and returned with the frock, which he spread reverently over the back of a chair.

"How perfectly sweet!" said my wife.

For a few moments he buried his head in his hands, and Alice and I were silent. I could not but observe the interesting mise-en-scene in which I found myself. The dim recesses of the room, heavy with memories. My wife cosily curled up in the high arm-chair, the firelight playing on her fresh, almost childlike, face, a simple ring sparkling on her finger, and on the pearly glint of her diaphanous gown. On the other side of the table where the little glasses stood, the clear-cut features and long snow-white hair of the old actor, silhouetted against a dark cabinet. And then, like some fragile ghost recalled to bear witness to its tragic past, the dim outline of the child's white frock.

"It was before your time, mes enfants, long, long before your time," he said suddenly. "You would not remember the famous Charles Carside Company who starred the provinces. We became known as the Capacity Company. The title was doubly-earned. We always played to full houses, and in those days-"

He turned to me with a penetrating, almost challenging look, and added: "There were actors.

Comedy, and tragedy, history, everything worth doing, in the legitimate, was in our repertoire. We changed our bill every night, and sometimes twice a day. Ay, and we changed our parts, sir. I remember Terry O'Bane and I reversing the parts of Othello and Iago on alternate nights for two weeks at a stretch. I played Lord Stamford to his Puttick in 'The Golden Dawn.' He played Shylock to my Bassanio. I will not bore you with these details. Ah! poor old Terry! Poor dear old Terry!"
He stopped and looked down at his hands, and neither of us spoke.

"When I say that Terry O'Bane and I were friends, I want to tell you that we were friends as only artists can be friends. We loved each other. For three years we worked together side by side—never a suspicion of envy, never a suspicion of jealousy. I remember one night, after Terry's delivery of Jaques' speech on the fool, he did not get a hand. I found him weeping in the wings. 'Old fellow!' I said, but he gripped me by the arm. 'Colly boy,' he answered, 'I was thinking of you. I knew how distressed you would be!'

Think of that! His only concern was that I should be distressed. Ah! in those days ... "

He stretched his long white fingers and examined them; then, turning suddenly to my wife, he said:

"I want to ask you, mademoiselle" (he persisted in calling her 'mademoiselle' all the evening), "to make allowances in what I am about to tell you for the tempora et mores. In my young days love had a different significance to what it has now. In this modern world I observe nothing but expediency and opportunism. No one is prepared to sacrifice, to run risks. The love between O'Bane and me was an epic of self-sacrifice, and it ran its full course. It found its acid test on the day when Sophie Wiles joined our company at Leeds."

He stood up, and his voice trembled in a low whisper. Looking at Alice, he said:

"She was as beautiful, as fragile, as adorable as you are, mademoiselle.

Strange how these great secrets are conveyed imperceptibly. O'Bane and I looked at each other, and instinctively we understood. We said nothing. We made no comment about her. We were entirely solicitous of each other's feelings. We referred to her as ' Miss Wiles ' and we addressed her as ' Miss Wiles.' Before we had been three weeks on the road I knew that if I had not known O'Bane's feelings I should have gone to her and said, ' Sophie, my darling, my angel, I love you, I adore you. Will you marry me?' But would it have been chivalrous to do this, knowing O'Bane's sentiments? We were two months on the road before the matter reached its climax. And during that time—under an unspoken compact—neither of us made love to Sophie. And then, one night, I could bear it no longer. I saw the drawn and hungry look in my colleague's eye as he watched her from the wings. I went up to him and whispered, 'Old fellow, go in and win. She's worthy of you.' He understood me at once, and he pressed my hand. 'Colly,' he said,' you're right. This can't go on. Meet me after the show and come round to my rooms.'"

The old actor's lips were trembling. He drew his chair nearer to my wife's. "I cannot tell you of the heart-burning interview I had with my old friend that night. Each tried to give way to the other. It was very terrible, very moving. At length we decided that the only solution would be to put the matter to a hazard. We could not cut cards or throw dice. It seemed profane. We decided to play a game of chess. We set out the pieces and began. But at the end of a few moments it was apparent that each was trying to let the other win. 'Stay,' I said; 'we must leave the verdict to impartial destiny, after all,' and I rose. On the sideboard—as it might be here was a large bowl of Gloire-de-Dijon roses. I took the largest bloom and said,' Terry, old boy, if there are an odd number of petals in this rose, she is yours. If an even number, I will pay her court.' He agreed. Slowly and deliberately, petal by petal, I destroyed the beautiful bloom. There were fifty-eight petals. When Terry saw the last petal fall he turned white and swayed. I helped him to the easy-chair and handed him a little grog. It was nearly dawn. Already the birds were twittering on the window-sill."

He turned and gazed at the window as though even now the magic of that early morning was upon him.

"The dawn was clear for me, but for my friend how dark and foreboding! Or so it seemed to both of us at that hour. But, as Mahomet said,' With women, life is a condition of flux.' At eleven o'clock that morning I was on my bended knees to Sophie. I poured out all my pent-up feelings of the two months. There are some things too sacred to repeat even to those who are—dear to us."

He gasped and, stretching out his arm, poured out another glass of the Chartreuse.

"She refused me, or if she did not actually refuse me—indeed, she did not; she was sympathetic, almost loving, but so—indeterminate that I was almost driven to a frenzy of despair. When one is young, one is like that. One must have all, and at once, or go crazy with despair. For a week I courted her day and night, and I could not make her decide. She liked me, but she did not love me. At the end of that time, I went to O'Bane, and I said, ' Old man, it is your call. My part is played.' Under great pressure from me he consented to enter the lists, and I withheld my hand as he had done. Even now the memory of that week of anguish when I knew that my greatest friend was making love to my adored is almost unbearable. At the end of the week he came to me and said, ' Old boy, I don't know how I stand. She likes me, but I hardly think she loves me.' I will not burden you with the chronicle of our strange actions which followed. We decided that as the question was identical it should be an open fight in a fair field, otherwise, between us, we should lose her altogether. We would both pay court to her wherever and whenever the opportunity occurred. And we would do so without animosity or ill-will. The tour lasted three months, and I knew that O'Bane was winning. There was no question about it. He was the favorite. Every minute I was expecting to hear the dread glad tidings. And then a strange thing happened."

He leant back in his chair and passed his hands through his hair with a graceful gesture.

"An uncle in Australia died and left O'Bane an enormous fortune. He was rich beyond the dreams of avarice. The company all knew of it, and were delighted, all—all except one person."

He glanced towards my wife, and sighed.

"I have lived a good many years, and yet I seem to find the heart of woman as unfathomable, as unexplorable as ever. They are to me the magic casements opening on the night. There is no limit . . . every subtle human experience is capable of endless variation. Sophie refused to marry O'Bane because people would think she married him for his money. The anguish of those last weeks I shall never forget. She definitely refused him, and I was torn between my love for O'Bane and my love for Sophie. I can say with perfect truth—literal truth—that the fortune killed O'Bane. When we arrived in London, he began to squander. He drank, gambled, and led a depraved life, all because the woman he loved would not marry him. In the spring he left the company and took a house in town. It became the happy hunting-ground of loose characters. It is needless to say that if Sophie wouldn't man-y him, there were plenty of other women willing to marry a young millionaire. He became entangled with a fast and pretty creature called Annabel Peacock. He married her, and in the following year they had a child."

The fire crackled on the hearth; my wife did not take her eyes from the old actor's face. A black cat strolled leisurely across the room and stretched itself before the fire. He continued:

"It was then that I experienced an entirely novel vision of woman's character. Sophie, who would not marry O'Bane because he was rich, and who shivered with disgust in the presence of Annabel Peacock, developed an amazing affection and interest for their child. We were out again in the Capacity Company. I had her all to myself. I laid siege to her heart. I was patient, tactful, importunate, imploring, passionate. But it was all no good, my boy ... no good at all. Heigho! would you believe it?—for ten years of my life from that date I was that woman's slave, and she was the slave of Terry's child. Company after company I joined in order to be with her. I gave up good parts. I sacrificed leads, and in fact I even accepted a walk-on—anything to be with Sophie. Sophie, who would not listen to me, who treated me like a little pet, to run hither and thither, and who spent all her money and time on toys and clothes for Terry's child. Would you believe it?"

To my surprise, my wife spoke for the first time. She said: "Yes." Brancker looked at her keenly, and nodded.

"Yes. In any affair between a man and a woman, a man finds himself at a disadvantage. Mademoiselle, you see, understands. Women have all kinds of mysterious intuitions and senses which we wot not of. She is armed at every point. She has more resources. She is better-equipped than man. Sophie even made a friend of Annabel. She wrote her loving letters and called her ' my dearest.' For you must know that two years after his marriage my old friend Terry O'Bane went under. He awakened one night feeling ill; he groped in a chest where he usually kept a flask of brandy. He took a gulp. The liquid he drew into his throat was pure liquid ammonia which Annabel had been using for photographic work. She was a keen amateur photographer. He rushed out into the street in his pajamas, and died in the arms of a policeman at the comer."

The honor of this episode was written plainly in the old man's face. He delivered it with a kind of dramatic despair, as though he knew it had to be told and he could not control himself. Then he seemed to fall to pieces, and lay huddled at the back of his chair. I looked at Alice furtively, and I could see a tear swimming on the brink of her eye. It was some moments before he could continue.

"These were all the best years of my life, mes enfants, when my powers were at their highest. My old friend Toole offered me a good part in London. He said to me, 'Brancker, old man, you're wasting yourself in the provinces. Come to town and take a lead.' I could only press his hand and thank him. In another week or two I was on the road again with Sophie. As the years went by she became more and more absorbed by Terry's unattractive child, and more and more distressed concerning it. For you must know that in spite of his profligate life, Terry still had left a considerable fortune, and Annabel continued to live in the same way. And it was the worst possible atmosphere to bring a child up in. Annabel was kind to the child in a spasmodic way, passionate and unreliable. She would pet it and coax it, and buy it expensive toys and dresses, and then suddenly neglect or scold it.

Sophie knew this, and all the time she could spare she went to London and tried to help the situation. She humored and flattered Annabel, who was quite manageable if you treated her like this, and she did what she could to influence the early training of the child for good. But, as you may imagine, the little minx grew up the spit and image of her mother. She was vain, fickle, and spoilt. By the time she was ten she thought of nothing but her looks and her frocks; and she was indeed a very pretty child. She had all the prettiness of her mother, with something of her father's grace and charm. She was encouraged to amuse the vulgar people who came to the house, and she was allowed to listen to all the loose talk, and to sit up to any hour she liked, unless Annabel happened to be in a contrary mood, when she would slap the child and lock her in her room.

"'Aunt Sophie,' as she called her, was a favorite with Lucy, but only, I'm afraid, because 'Aunt Sophie' gave her expensive toys, and lavished her love persistently upon the child. She wrote to her nearly every day, wherever she happened to be, and sent her little gifts."

The old man mopped his forehead. He was evidently laboring under the severe strain which the invoking of these memories put upon him. He walked to the sideboard and poured himself out a glass of water, into which he poured- an as after-thought—a tiny drop of rum. After taking two long, meditative gulps, he resumed his seat. He seemed to have forgotten all about our presence. He was living in the past. But suddenly he turned to my wife and said:

"I have many of the beautiful frocks which Sophie made for little Lucy. They have come down to me. If it would not bore you to call one afternoon, mademoiselle, I could show you some that might interest you." There was a strange, eager appeal in his voice. It seemed a matter of tremendous moment that Alice should go and inspect the frocks. My heart bled for him. "Of course she will go," I thought, but to my surprise, she said nothing. She just looked at him with that queer, watchful expression that women alone arc capable of. Perhaps it is part of what the old chap referred to—their equipment. She toyed with the chain on her frock, and his eye meditated her movements. He hesitated, and then rather nervously proceeded, as though talking to himself.

"Frocks! What a part they play in our lives. Carlyle was right. Sophie was extraordinarily clever with her needle. She had a genius for combining materials. Her theatrical experience helped her. She made the most alluring frocks. The child adored' Aunt Sophie's' frocks. They always looked so striking and so professional. The crisis in my life, and which I am about to tell you of, was indeed occasioned by one of the frocks which Sophie made for Lucy. It came about in this way."
He paused again, and tapped the top of the table with his beautiful white hands.

"That last year—that year when Lucy reached her tenth birthday—the excesses in Annabel's house reached their zenith. The place became notorious. Annabel had taken to herself a drunken lord. Lord Starborough. He was a dissipated young roue. He rather took a fancy to Lucy, and he spoilt her in the same way that Annabel did. We heard stories of the goings on. The child was taken to houses to dance. I believe she was even taught to put on rouge. There was a rich family called the Arkwrights, who also had children, and who lived a similar life. These children were Lucy's great friends. They vied with each other in their infantile snobbery. The parents gave elaborate parties and tried to outshine each other in the lavish-ness of their entertainment, and the overdressing of the children. It was very, very painful. Even I, whose life was being wrecked by Sophie's adulation of this child, felt sorry. My heart bled for my old friend's daughter.

"We had a long tour that autumn, Sophie and I. We were out in' The Woman Who Failed.' Sophie had a lead, but I was only playing the part of a butler. It was a long and trying tour up North. The weather was very bitter. There was a good deal of sickness, and our chief was a hard man. Early in December Sophie caught a cold which rapidly developed into bronchitis. She had a narrow escape.

She was, however, only out of the bill for ten days. She insisted on returning and struggling on. The tour was to end on Christmas Eve. One day she had a letter from Lucy. I remember the exact words to this day. ' Dear Aunt Sophie, do make me a lovely frock for Christmas Eve. The Arkwrights are having a lovely ball, and I know Irene is having a gold and green, with a sparkling veil. Your loving Lucy.'

"When Sophie got this letter she smiled. She was happy. She was always happy when doing a service. Ah! me .... For nearly a week she thought and dreamt about the frock she was going to make for Lucy for the Arkwrights' party. She knew what the child wanted—a frock to outshine all the others. Then another story reached us. I have forgotten what it was: some distressing record of these Arkwright people. One night after the show she sent for me. I could tell she was very agitated.

She clutched my arm, and said, 'Old man, I know what I'm going to do. I'm going to make Lucy a frock which will outshine all the others. And it will be just plain white frock, with no adornment of any sort. Just think of it, amongst all those vulgar, overdressed children, one little girl, as pretty as Lucy, in plain white. And they will be bound to appreciate it. It will tell. And perhaps she will realize-what it means. Good taste and refinement will always tell against vulgarity.'

I applauded Sophie's idea, and I went with her to get the material. But she fainted in the shop. During those last few days I began to realize that Sophie was very ill. She was simply living on her nervous force, keeping herself going in order to complete the tour, and to deliver Lucy's frock in time for the ball.

"Our last journey back was from Nottingham. We arrived in London at five o'clock on Christmas Eve. I was in a fever of dread. I believed that Sophie was dying. She kept swaying in the train as though she was going to drop. Her face was deadly-white, her eyes unnaturally bright, and her fingers were still busy on the frock. So absorbed had I been in Sophie's affairs, I had made no arrangements about lodgings in town. Neither had she. But my old friend, Joe Cadgers, seeing my distress, said,' Old boy, leave it to me. I know a snug little place where they'll take you in. I'm not stopping. I'm going straight through to Hastings.' I thanked my old friend and embraced him. When we got to Euston, we got Sophie into a four-wheeled cab, and Joe Gadgers came with us to arrange the introduction. I hardly noticed where the lodgings were—somewhere in Clapham, I think. We arrived there, and a good lady took us in without hesitation. We put Sophie to bed. She was almost delirious, but still the frock was not quite finished. Joe left us, and I sat by her bedside, watching her busy fingers. I knew it was useless to protest. The clock on the mantelpiece ticked, and outside the snow was beginning to fall."

Colin Brancker stood up, and suddenly picked up the little white frock from the back of the chair. He held it in his arms reverently and tenderly. His voice was strong and resonant. He stood there, and acted the scene vividly before our eyes.

"At ten minutes to seven I left the house, holding the frock in my arms. I rushed out without a hat, without a coat. I flew along the street, calling out for a cab like a madman .... At last I got one. I told the driver to drive like the furies to the address I gave him in Kensington. In the cab I stamped my feet and rocked the dress in my arms as though it were a fevered child. I don't know how we got there. It seemed an eternity. I flung into the house, calling out, 'Lucy! Lucy!' I found her in the drawing-room. She was dressed in a flaming orange and silver dress, with a sparkling tiara in her hair. She was looking in a mirror and putting finishing touches to her hair.

She cried out when she saw me: "Hullo! I thought Aunt Sophie had forgotten me. I've hired a frock from Roco's.' 'Child,' I said, 'your Aunt Sophie has been working out her life's blood for you. Here is the frock.' She grabbed it and examined it. 'Frock!' she said. 'It looks more like a nightdress. I don't want the beastly old thing'; and she threw it across the room. I believe at that moment I could have struck the child. I was blind with fury. Fortunately, I remembered in time that she was my old friend Terry O'Bane's daughter. I picked up the frock.

'Ungrateful child!' I exclaimed. 'You don't know what you're doing. You're murdering an ideal. You're killing your aunt.' She tossed her insolent head and actually pressed the bell for the butler to see me out. Just like a grown-up person. Dazed and baffled, I clutched the little white frock and staggered out into the street. The night was dark, and the snow was still falling. Christmas bells were beginning to peal....I plunged on and on, my heart beating against my ribs. People stared at me, but I was too distressed to care. How could I go back to Sophie with the insulting message? Suddenly, at the corner of Hyde Park, a most appalling realization flashed through my mind. I had made no note of the address of the lodgings where Sophie and I were staying! ... God in heaven! What was I to do? The only man who could help me, my old friend, Joe Gadgers, had gone to Hastings. What could I do? Could I go to the police and say, 'Will you help me to find the address of some lodgings where an actress is staying? I think it's somewhere round about Clapham. I don't know the name of the landlady, or the name of the street, or the number?' They would have thought I was mad. Perhaps I was mad. Should I go back to Lucy? The child wouldn't know .... And all this time Sophie was dying. Ah! merciful God! perhaps she would die. If she died before I found her, she would die in the happy belief that the frock had been worn. Her last hours would be blessed with dreams, visions of purity and joy ... whilst I ... I should have no place in them, perhaps ... but I, too, after all, I'd suffered for her sake. Who knows? ... Who know ...?"

His voice broke off in a low sob. I leant forward watching his face, racked with anguish. The room was extraordinarily still .... I dared not look at Alice, but I was conscious of the pearly sheen of her frock under the lamp. Away in the distance one could hear the rumble of the traffic on the High-road. The remorseless tick of the clock was the only sound in the room. Once I thought it ticked louder, and then I realized that it was some one tapping gently at the door. The door opened a little way, and against the dim light in the passage appeared the gaunt face of the old serving-woman, phantom-like, unreal ....

"Excuse me, sir." She peered into the room. The old actor gazed at her with unseeing eyes. He stood with one hand on the back of the chair, and across the other arm lay the white frock; a dignified and pathetic figure.

"I'm sorry to trouble you, sir,"

"Yes, Mrs. Windsor?"

"My little niece 'as just called. I can't find it anywhere—that little frock I made for 'er last week. I put it in the chest. I thought perhaps you might 'ave ... Oh! there it is, sir. Do you mind-? Thank you very much, sir. I'm sorry to have disturbed the company."

In the sanctuary of our bedroom that night, my wife said:

"Did you really believe that that writing on the photograph was by Henry Irving?"

"My dear," I answered, "When their careers are finished, the painter, the author, the architect or the sculptor may point to this or that, and say, 'Lo! this is my handiwork.' But to the actor nothing remains but—memories. Their permanence lies in the memories of those who loved them. Are we to begrudge them all the riches of imagination? After all, what is the line of demarcation between what we call reality and what we call imagination? Is not the imagery invoked by Shelley when he sings of dubious myths as real a fact as the steel rivets in the Forth Bridge? What is reality? Indeed, what is life?"

"I don't know what life is," answered my wife, switching off the light. "But I know what you are. You're a dear old—perfect old—BOOB!"

"Alice, what do you mean?" I said.

She laughed softly.

"Women are 'equipped,' you know," she replied enigmatically, and insisted on going to sleep.

A Good Action

It is undoubtedly true that the majority of us perform the majority of our actions through what are commonly known as mixed motives. It would certainly have been quite impossible for Mr. Edwin Pothecary to analyze the concrete impulse which eventually prompted him to perform his good action. It may have been a natural revolt from the somewhat petty and cramped punctilio of his daily life; his drab home life, the bickering, wearing, grasping routine of the existence of fish-and-chips dispenser. A man who earns his livelihood by buying fish and potatoes in the cheapest market, and selling them in the Waterloo Road cannot afford to indulge his altruistic fancies to any lavish extent. It is true that the business of Mr. Edwin Pothecary was a tolerably successful one—he employed three assistants and a boy named Scales who was not so much an assistant as an encumbrance and wholesale plate-smasher. Mr. Pothecary engaged him because he thought his name seemed appropriate to the fish-trade. In a weak moment he pandered to this sentimental whim, another ingredient in the strange composition which influences us to do this, that, and the other. But it was not by pandering to whims of this nature that Mr. Pothecary had built up this progressive and odoriferous business with its gay shop front of blue and brown tiles. It was merely a minor lapse. In the fish-and-chip trade one has to be keen, pushful, self-reliant, ambidexterous, a student of human nature, forbearing, far-seeing, imaginative, courageous, something of a controversialist with a streak of fatalism as pronounced as that of a high-priest in a Brahmin temple. It is better, moreover, to have an imperfect nasal organism, and to be religious.

Edwin had all these qualities. Every day he went from Quince Villa at Buffington to London—forty minutes in the train—and back at night. On Sunday he took the wife and three children to the Methodist Chapel at the comer of the street to both morning and evening services. But even this religious observance does not give us a complete solution for the sudden prompting of an idea to do a good action. Edwin had attended chapel for fifty-two years and such an impulse had never occurred to him before. He may possibly have been influenced by some remark of the preacher, or was it that twinge of gout which set him thinking of the unwritten future? Had it anything to do with the Boy-Scout movement? Some one at some time had told him of an underlying idea—that every day in one's life one should do one pure, good and unselfish action.

Perhaps after all it was all due to the gayety of a spring morning. Certain it is that as he swung out of the garden gate on that morning in April something stirred in him. His round puffy face blinked heavenwards. Almond blossoms fluttered in the breeze above the hedgerows. Larks were singing .... Suddenly his eye alighted upon the roof of the Peels' hen-house opposite and Mr. Edwin Pothecary scowled.

Lose confidence in that splendid gold-lettered tablet in the window which said "Cod, brill, halibut, plaice, pilchards always on hand. Eat them or take them away."

The latter sentence did not imply that if you took them away you did not eat them; it simply meant that you could either stand at the counter and eat them from a plate with the aid of a fork and your fingers (or at one of the wooden benches if you could find room—an unlikely contingency, alternatively you could wrap them up in a piece of newspaper and devour them without a fork at the comer of the street.

No, it would not be a good action in any way to close the Popular Plaice to eat. Edwin came to the conclusion that to perform this act satisfactorily it were better to divorce the proceeding entirely from any connection with home or business. The two things didn't harmonize. A good action must be a special and separate effort in an entirely different setting. He would take the day off himself and do it thoroughly.

Mr. Pothecary was known in the neighborhood of the Waterloo Road as "The Stinker," a title easily earned by the peculiar qualities of his business and the obvious additional fact that a Pothecary was a chemist. He was a very small man, bald-headed with yellowy-white side whiskers, a blue chin, a perambulating nostril with a large wart on the port side. He wore a square bowler hat which seemed to thrust out the protruding flaps of his large ears. His greeny-black clothes were always too large for him and ended in a kind of thick spiral above his square-toed boots. He always wore a flat white collar—more or less clean—and no tie. This minor defect was easily atoned for by a heavy silver chain on his waistcoat from which hung gold seals and ribbons connecting with watches, knives, and all kinds of ingenious appliances in his waistcoat pockets.

The noble intention of his day was a little chilled on his arrival at the shop. In the first place, although customers were then arriving for breakfast, the boy Scales was slopping water over the front step. Having severely castigated the miscreant youth and prophesied that his chances of happiness in the life to come were about as remote as those of a dead dog-fish in the upper reaches of the Thames, he made his way through the customers to the room at the back, and there he met Dolling.

Dolling was Edwin's manager, and he cannot be overlooked. In the first place, he was remarkably like a fish himself. He had the same dull expressionless eyes and the drooping mouth and drooping mustache. Everything about him drooped and dripped. He was always wet. He wore a gray flannel shirt and no collar or tie. His braces, trousers, and hair all seemed the same color. He hovered in the background with a knife, and did the cutting up and dressing. He had, moreover, all the taciturnity of a fish, and its peculiar ability for getting out of a difficulty. He never spoke. He simply looked lugubrious, and pointed at things with his knife. And yet Edwin knew that he was an excellent manager. For it must be observed that in spite of the gold-lettered board outside with its fanfare of cod, brill, halibut, plaice and pilchards, whatever the customer asked for, by the time it had passed through Boiling's hand it was just fish. No nonsense about it at all. Just plain fish leveled with a uniform brown crust. If you asked for cod you got fish. If you asked for halibut you also got fish. Dolling was something of an artist.

On this particular morning, as Edward entered the back room, Dolling was scratching the side of his head with the knife he used to cut up the fish; a sure sign that he was perplexed about something. It was not customary to exchange greetings in this business, and when he observed "the guv'nor" enter he just withdrew the knife from his hair and pointed it at a packing case on the side table. Edwin knew what this meant. He went up and pressed his flat nose against the chest of what looked like an over-worked amphibian that had been turned down by its own Trades Union. Edwin sneezed before he had had time to withdraw his nose.

"Yes, that's a dud lot," he said. And then suddenly an inspirational moment nearly overwhelmed him. Here was a chance. He would turn to Dolling and say:

"Dolling, this fish is slightly tainted. We must throw it away. We bought it at our risk. Yesterday morning when it arrived it was just all right, but keeping it in that hot room downstairs where you and your wife sleep has probably finished it. We mustn't give it to our customers. It might poison them—ptomaine poison, you know ... eh. Dolling?"

It would be a good action, a self-sacrificing action, eh? But when he glanced at the face of Dolling he knew that such an explosion would be unthinkable. I would be like telling a duck it mustn't swim, or an artist that he mustn't paint, or a boy on a beach that he mustn't throw stones in the sea. It was the kind of job that Dolling enjoyed. In the course of a few hours he knew quite well that whatever he said, the mysterious and evil-smelling monster would be served out in dainty parcels of halibut, cod, brill, plaice, etc.

Business was no place for a good action. Too many others depended on it, were involved in it. Edwin went up to Dolling and shouted in his ear—he was rather deaf:

"I'm going out. I may not be back to-day."

Dolling stared at the wall. He appeared about as interested in the statement as a cod might be that had just been informed that a Chinese coolie had won the Calcutta sweep-stake. Edwin crept out of the shop abashed. He felt horribly uncomfortable. He heard some one mutter: "Where's The Stinker off to?" and he realized how impossible it would be to explain to any one there present that he was off to do a good action.

"I will go to some outlying suburb," he thought.

Once outside in the sunshine he tried to get back into the benign mood. He traveled right across London and made for Golders Green and Heudon, a part of the world foreign to him. By the time he had boarded the Golders Green 'bus he had quite recovered himself. It was still a brilliant day. "The better the day the better the deed," he thought aptly. He hummed inaudibly; that is to say, he made curious crooning noises somewhere behind his silver chain and signets; the sound was happily suppressed by the noise of the 'bus.

It seemed a very long journey. It was just as they were going through a rather squalid district near Cricklewood that the golden chance occurred to him. The fares had somewhat thinned. There were scarcely a dozen people in the 'bus. Next to him barely a yard away he observed a poor woman with a baby in her arms. She had a thin, angular, wasted face, and her clothes were threadbare but neat. A poor, thoroughly honest and deserving creature, making a bitter fight of it against the buffets of a cruel world. Edwin's heart was touched. Here was his chance. He noticed that from her wrist was suspended a shabby black bag, and the bag was open. He would slip up near her and drop in a half-crown. What joy and rapture when she arrived home and found the unexpected treasure! An unknown benefactor! Edwin chuckled and wormed his way surreptitiously along the seat. Stealthily he fingered his half-crown and hugged it in the palm of his left hand. His heart beat with the excitement of his exploit. He looked out of the window opposite and fumbled his hand towards the opening in the bag. He touched it. Suddenly a sharp voice rang out:

"That man's picking your pocket!"

An excited individual opposite was pointing at him. The woman uttered an exclamation and snatched at her bag. The baby cried. The conductor rang the bell. Every one seemed to be closing in on Edwin. Instinctively he snatched his hand away and thrust it in his pocket (the most foolish thing he could have done). Every one was talking. A calm muscular-looking gentleman who had not spoken seized Edwin by the wrist and said calmly:

"Look in your bag, Madam, and see whether he has taken anything." The 'bus came to a halt. Edwin muttered:

"I assure you—nothing of the sort—"

How could he possibly explain that he was doing just the opposite? Would a single person believe a word of his yam about the half-crown? The woman whimpered:

"No, 'e ain't taken nothin', bad luck to 'im. There was only four pennies and a 'alfpenny anyway. Dirty thief!"

"Are you goin' to give 'im in charge?" asked the conductor.

"Yer can't if 'e ain't actually taken nothin', can yer? The dirty thievin' swine try in' to rob a 'ard workin' 'onest woman!"

"I wasn't! I wasn't!" feebly spluttered Edwin, blushing a ripe beetroot color. "Shame! Shame! Chuck 'im off the 'bus! Dirty sneak! Call a copper!" were some of the remarks being hurled about.

The conductor was losing time and patience. He beckoned vigorously to Edwin and said:

"Come on, off you go!"

There was no appeal. He got up and slunk out. Popular opinion was too strong against him. As he stepped off the back board, the conductor gave him a parting kick which sent him flying on to the pavement. It was an operation received with shrieks of laughter and a round of applause from the occupants of the vehicle, taken up by a small band of other people who had been attracted by the disturbance. He darted down a back street to the accompaniment of boos and jeers.

It says something for Edwin Pothecary that this unfortunate rebuff to his first attempt to do a good action did not send him helter-skelter back to the fried fish shop in the Waterloo Road. He felt crumpled, bruised, mortified, disappointed, discouraged; but is not the path of all martyrs and reformers strewn with similar debris? Are not all really disinterested actions liable to misconstruction? He went into a dairy and partook of a glass of milk and a bun. Then he started out again. He would see more rural, less sophisticated people. In the country there must be simple, kindly people, needing his help. He walked for several hours with but a vague sense of direction. At last he came to a public park. A group of dirty boys were seated on the grass. They were apparently having a banquet.

They did not seem to require him. He passed on, and came to an enclosure. Suddenly between some rhododendron bushes he looked into a small dell. On a seat by himself was an elderly man in a shabby suit. He looked the picture of misery and distress. His hands were resting on his knees, and his eyes were fixed in a melancholy scrutiny on the ground. It was obvious that some great trouble obsessed him. He was as still as a shadow. It was the figure of a man lost in the past or—contemplating suicide? Edwin's breath came quickly. He made his way to him. In order to do this it was necessary to climb a railing. There was probably another way round, but was there time? At any minute there might be a sudden movement, the crack of a revolver. Edwin tore his trousers and scratched his forearm, but he managed to enter the dell unobserved. He approached the seat. The man never looked up. Then Edwin said with sympathetic tears in his voice:

"My poor fellow, may I be of any assistance—?"

There was a disconcerting jar. The melancholy individual started and turned on him angrily: "Blast you! I'd nearly got it! What the devil are you doing here?"

And without waiting for an answer he darted away among the trees. At the same time a voice called over the park railings:

"Ho! you, there, what are you doing over there? You come back the way you came. I sawyer."

The burly figure of a park-keeper with gaiters and stout stick beckoned him. Edwin got up and clambered back again, scratching his arm.

"Now then" said the keeper. "Name, address, age, and occupation, if you please."

"I was only—" began Edwin. But what was he only doing? Could he explain to a park-keeper that he was only about to do a kind action to a poor man? He spluttered and gave his name, address, age, and occupation.

"Oh," exclaimed the keeper. "Fried fish, eh? And what were you trying to do? Get orders? Or were you begging from his lordship?"

"His lordship?"

"That man you was speaking to was Lord Budleigh-Salterton, the great scientist. He's thinkin' out 'is great invention, otherwise I'd go and ask him if 'e wanted to prosecute yer for being in 'is park on felonious intent or what."

"I assure you—"stammered Mr. Pothecary.

The park-keeper saw him well off the premises, and gave him much gratuitous advice about his future behavior, darkened with melancholy prophecies regarding the would-be felon's strength of character to live up to it.

Leaving the park he struck out towards the more rural neighbourhood. He calculated that he must be somewhere in the neighborhood of Hendon. At the end of a lane he met a sallow-faced young man walking rapidly. His eyes were bloodshot and restless. He glanced at Edwin and stopped. "Excuse me, sir," he said.

Edwin drew himself to attention. The young man looked up and down nervously. He was obviously in a great state of distress.

"What can I do for you? "

"I—I—h-hardly like to ask you, sir, I—"

He stammered shockingly. Edwin turned on his most sympathetic manner. "You are suffering. What is it? "

"Sh-Sh-Shell-shock, shir."

"Ah!"

At last! Some heroic reflex of the war darted through Edwin's mind. Here was his real chance at last. A poor fellow broken by the war and in need, neglected by an ungrateful country. Almost hidden by his outer coat he observed one of those little strips of colored ribbon, which implied more than one campaign.

"Where did you meet your trouble?" he asked.

"P—P—P-Palestine, sir, capturing a T-T-Turkish redoubt. I was through Gallipoli, too, sir, but I won't d-d-distress you. I am in a—in a—hospital at St. Albans, came to see my g-g-g-girl, but she's g-g-g-gone—v-v-vanished ... "

"You don't say so!"

"T-t-trouble is I I-I-I-lost my p-pass back. N-not quite enough m-mon—"

"Dear me! How much short are you?"

"S-S-S-Six shill—S-S-S-Six—"

"Six shillings? Well, I'm very sorry. Look here, my good fellow, here's seven-and-sixpence and God bless you!"

"T—T—thank you very much, sir. W—will you give me your n—name and—"

"No, no, no, that's quite all right. I'm very pleased to be of assistance. Please, forget all about it."'

He pressed the soldier's hand and hurried on. It was done. He had performed a kind, unselfish action and no one should ever hear of it. Mr. Pothecary's eyes glowed with satisfaction. Poor fellow! even if the story were slightly exaggerated, what did it matter? He was obviously a discharged soldier, ill, and in need. The seven-and-sixpence would make an enormous difference. He would always cherish the memory of his kind, unknown benefactor. It was a glorious sensation! Why had he never thought of doing a kindly act? It was inspiring, illuminating, almost intoxicating! He recalled with zest the delirious feeling which ran through him when he said, "No, no, no!" He would not give his name. He was the good Samaritan, a ship passing in the night. And now he would be able to go home, or go back to his business. He swung down the lane, singing to himself. As he turned the comer he came to a low bungalow-building. It was in a rather deserted spot. It had a board outside which announced "Tea, cocoa, light refreshments. Cyclists catered for."

It was past mid-day, and although tea and cocoa had never made any great appeal to the gastronomic fancies of Edwin Pothecary, he felt in his present spiritually elevated mood that here was a suitable spot for a well-merited rest and lunch.

He entered a deserted 'room, filled with light oak chairs, and tables with green-tiled tops on which were placed tin vases containing dried ferns. A few bluebottles darted away from the tortuous remains of what had once apparently been a ham, lurking behind tall bottles of sweets on the counter. The room smelt of soda and pickles. Edwin rapped on the table for some time, but no one came. At last a woman entered from the front door leading to the garden. She was fat and out of breath.

Edwin coughed and said:

"Good-mornin', madam. May I have a bite of some-thin'?"

The woman looked at him and continued panting. When her pulmonary contortions had somewhat subsided she said:

"I s'pose you 'aven't seen a pale young man up the lane?"

It was difficult to know what made him do it, but Edwin lied. He said: "No."

"Oh!" she replied. "I don't know where 'e's got to. 'E's not s'posed to go out of the garden. 'E's been ill, you know."

"Really!"

"'E's my nefyer, but I can't always keep an eye on 'im. 'E's a bright one, 'e is. I shall 'ave 'im sent back to the 'ome."

"Ah, poor fellow! I suppose he was—injured in the war?"

"War!" The plump lady snorted. She became almost aggressive and confidential. She came close up to Edwin and shook her finger backwards and forwards in front of his eyes.

"I'll tell yer 'ow much war 'e done. When they talked about conscription, 'e got that frightened, 'e went out every day and tried to drink himself from a A1 man into a C III man, and by God! 'e succeeded."

"You don't say so!"

"I do say so. And more. When 'is turn came, 'e was in the 'orspital with Delirious Trimmings."

"My God!"

"'E's only just come out. 'E's all right as long as 'e don't get 'old of a little money."

"What do you mean?"

"If 'e can get 'old of the price of a few whiskies, 'e'll 'ave another attack come on! What are yer goin' ter 'ave—tea or cocoa?"

"I must go! I must go!" exclaimed the only customer Mrs. Boggins had had for two days, and gripping his umbrella he dashed out of the shop.

"Good Lord! there's another one got 'em!" ejaculated the good landlady. "I wonder whether 'e pinched anything while I was out? 'Ere! Come back, you dirty little bow-legged swipe!"

But Mr. Pothecary was racing down the lane, muttering to himself: "Yes, that was a good action! A very good action indeed!"

A mile further on he came to a straggling village, a forlorn unkempt spot, only relieved by a gaudy inn called "The Two Tumblers." Edwin staggered into the private bar and drank two pints of Government ale and a double gin as the liquid accompaniment to a hunk of bread and cheese.

It was not till he had lighted his pipe after the negotiation of these delicacies that he could again focus his philosophical outlook. Then he thought to himself: "It's a rum thing 'ow difficult it is to do a good action. You'd think it'd be dead easy, but everythin' seems against yer. One must be able to do it somewhere. P'raps one ought to go abroad, among foreigners and black men. That's it! That's why all these 'ere Bible Society people go out among black people, Chinese and so on. They find there's nothin' doin' over 'ere."

Had it not been for the beer and gin it is highly probable that Edwin would have given up the project, and have returned to fish and chips. But lying back in a comfortable seat in "The Two Tumblers" his thoughts mellowed. He felt broad-minded, comfortable, tolerant ... one had to make allowances. There must be all sorts of ways. Money wasn't the only thing. Besides, he was spending too much. He couldn't afford to go on throwing away seven-and-six-pences. One must be able to help people—by helping them. Doing things for them which didn't cost money. He thought of Sir Walter R Raleigh throwing down his cloak for Queen Elizabeth to walk over. Romantic but—extravagant and silly, really a shrewd political move, no doubt; not a good action at all. If he met an ill-clad tramp he could take off his coat and wrap round his shoulders and then-? Walk home to Quince Villa in his braces? What would Mrs. Pothecary have to say? Phew! One could save people from drowning, but he didn't know how to swim. Fire! Perhaps there would be a fire. He could swarm up a ladder and save a woman from the top bedroom window. Heroic, but hardly inconspicuous; not exactly what he had meant. Besides, the firemen would never let him; they always kept these showy stunts for themselves. There must be something....

He walked out of "The Two Tumblers." Crossing the road, he took a turning off the High Street. He saw a heavily-built woman carrying a basket of washing. He hurried after her, and raising his hat, said: "Excuse me, madam, may I carry your basket for you?"

She turned on him suspiciously and glared: "No, thanks, Mr. Bottle-nose. I've 'ad some of that before. You 'op it! Mrs. Jaggs 'ad 'ers pinched last week that way."

"Of course," he thought to himself as he hurried away. "The trouble is I'm not dressed for the part. A bloomin' swell can go about loin' good actions all day and not arouse suspicions. If I try and 'elp a girl off a tram-car I get my face slapped."

Mr. Pothecary was learning. He was becoming a complete philosopher, but it was not till late in the afternoon that he suddenly realized that patience and industry are always rewarded. He was appealed to by a maiden in distress.

It came about in this way. He found the atmosphere of Northern London entirely unsympathetic to good deeds. All his action appeared suspect. He began to feel at last like a criminal. He was convinced that he was being watched and followed. Once he patted a little girl's head in a paternal manner. Immediately a woman appeared at a doorway and bawled out:

"'Ere, Lizzie, you come inside!"

At length in disgust he boarded a south-bound 'bus. He decided to experiment nearer home. He went to the terminus and took a train to the station just before his own. It was a small town called Uplingham. This should be the last dance of the moral philanderer. If there was no one in Uplingham upon whom he could perform a good action, he would just walk home—barely two miles—and go to bed and forget all about it. To-morrow he would return to Fish-and-chips, and the normal behavior of the normal citizen.

Uplingham was a dismal little town, consisting mostly of churches, chapels and pubs, and apparently quite deserted. As Edwin wandered through it there crept over him a sneaking feeling of relief. If he met no one—well, there it was, he had done his best; and he could go home with a clear conscience. After all it was the spirit that counted in these things ....

"o-o-oh!"

He was passing a small stone church, standing back on a little frequented lane. The maiden was seated alone in the porch and she was crying. Edwin bustled through the gate and as he approached her he had time to observe that she was young, quietly dressed, and distinctly pretty.

"You are in trouble," he said in his most feeling manner. She looked up at him quickly, and dabbed her eyes.

"I've lost my baby! I've lost my baby!" she cried.

"Dear, dear, that's very unfortunate! How did it happen?" She pointed at an empty perambulator in the porch.

"I waited an hour here for my friends and husband and the clergyman. My baby was to be christened." She gasped incoherently. "No one turned up. I went across to the Vicarage. The Vicar was away. I believe I ought to have gone to St. Bride's. This is St. Paul's. They didn't know anything about it. They say people often make that mistake." When I got back the baby was gone.

O-O-O-oh!"

"There, there, don't cry," said Mr. Pothecary. "Now I'll go over to St. Bride's and find out about it."

"Oh, sir, do you mind waiting here with the perambulator while I go? I want my baby. I want my baby."

"Why, yes, of course, of course."

She dashed up the lane and left Mr. Pothecary in charge of an empty perambulator. In fifteen minutes' time a thick-set young man came hurrying up to the porch. He looked at Edwin and pointing to the perambulator said:

"Is this Mrs. Frank's or Mrs. Fred's?"

"I don't know," said Edwin, rather testily.

"You don't know! But you're old Binns, ain't you?"

"No, I'm not."

The young man looked at him searchingly and then disappeared. Ten minutes elapsed and then a small boy rode up on a bicycle. He was also out of breath.

"Has Mrs. George been 'ere?" he asked. "I don't know," replied Edwin.

"Mr. Henderson says he's awfully sorry but he won't be able to get away. You are to kiss the baby for 'im."

"I don't know anything about it."

"This is St. Bride's, isn't it?"

"No, this is St. Paul's."

"Oh!" The boy leapt on to the bicycle and also vanished.

"This is absurd," thought Edwin. "Of course, the whole thing is as plain as daylight. The poor girl has come to the wrong church. The whole party is at St. Bride's, somebody must have taken the baby on there. I might as well take the perambulator along. They'll be pleased. Now I wonder which is the way."

He wheeled the perambulator into the lane. There was no one about to ask. He progressed nearly two hundred yards till he came to a field with a pond in it. This was apparently the wrong direction. He was staring about when he suddenly became aware of a hue and cry. A party of people came racing down the lane headed by the thick-set man, who was exclaiming:

"There he is! There he is!"

Edwin felt his heart beating. This was going to be a little embarrassing. They closed on him. The thickset man seized his wrists and at the same time remarked:

"See he hasn't any firearms on him, Frank."

The large man alluded to as Frank gripped him from behind.

"What have you done with my baby?" he demanded fiercely.

"I 'aven't seen no baby," yelped Mr. Pothecary.

"Oh! 'Aven't yer! What are yer doin' with my perambulator then?"

"I'm takin' it to St. Bride's Church."

"Goin' in the opposite direction."

"I didn't know the way."

"Where's the baby?"

"I 'aven't seen it. I tell yer. The mother said she'd lost it."

"What the hell! Do you know the mother's in bed sick? You're a liar, my man, and we're goin' to take you in charge. If you've done anything to my baby I'll kill you with my hands."

"That's it, Frank. Let 'im 'ave it. Throw 'im in the pond!"

"I tell yer I don't know anythin' about it all, with yer Franks, Freds and Georges! Go to the devil, all of yer!"

In spite of his protestations, some one produced a rope and they handcuffed him and tied him to the gate of the field. A small crowd had collected and began to boo and jeer. A man from a cottage hard by produced a drag, and between them they dragged the pond, as the general belief was that Edwin had tied a stone to the baby and thrown it in and was then just about to make off.

The uproar continued for some time, mud and stones being thrown about rather carelessly.

The crowd became impatient that no baby was found in the pond. At length another man turned up on a bicycle and called out:

"What are you doing, Frank? You've missed the christening!"

"What!"

"Old Binns turned up with the nipper all right. He'd come round the wrong way."

The crowd was obviously disappointed at the release of Edwin, and the father's only solatium was:

"Well, it's lucky for you, old bird!"

He and his friends trundled the perambulator away rapidly across the fields. Edwin had hardly time to give a sigh of relief before he found himself the center of a fresh disturbance. He was approaching the church when another crowd assailed him, headed by the forlorn maiden. She was still in a state of distress, but she was hugging a baby to her.

"Ah! You've found the baby!" exclaimed Edwin, trying to be amiable.

"Where is the perambulator?" she demanded.

"Your 'usband 'as taken it away, madam. He seemed to think I—"

A tall frigid young man stepped forward and said:

"Excuse me, I am the lady's husband. Will you please explain yourself?"

Then Edwin lost his temper.

"Well, damn it, I don't know who you all are!"

"The case is quite clear. You volunteered to take charge of the perambulator while my wife was absent. On her return you announce that it is spirited away. I shall hold you responsible for the entire cost—nearly ten pounds."

"Make it a thousand" roared Edwin. "I'm 'aving a nice cheap day."

"I don't wish for any more of your insolence, either. My wife has had a very trying experience. The baby has been christened Fred."

"Well, what's the matter with that?"

"Nothing," screamed the mother." Only that it is a girl! It's a girl and it has been duly christened Fred in a Christian church., Oh! there's been an awful muddle."

"It's not this old fool's fault," interpolated the elderly woman quietly. "You see, Mrs. Frank and Mrs. Fred Smith were both going to have their babies christened to-day. Only Mrs. Frank was took sick, and sent me along with the child. I went to the wrong church and thinkin' there was some mistake, went back home. Mrs. Frank's baby's never been christened at all. In the meantime, the ceremony was ready to start at St. Paul's and Frank 'isself was there. No baby. They sends old Binns to scout around at other churches.

People do make mistakes—finds this good lady's child all primed up for christening in the church door, and no one near, carries it off. In the meantime, the father had gone on the ramp. It's him that probably went off with the perambulator and trounced you up a bit, old sport. It'll learn you not to interfere so much in future perhaps."

"And the baby's christened Fred!" wailed the mother. "My baby! My Gwendoline!"

And she looked at Edwin with bitter recrimination in her eyes.

There was still a small crowd following and boys were jeering, and a fox terrier, getting very excited, jumped up and bit Mr. Pothecary through the seat of his trousers. He struck at it with his stick, and hit a small boy, whose mother happened to be present. The good lady immediately entered the lists.

"Baby-killer .... Hun!" were the last words he heard as he was chased up the street and across the fields in the direction of his own village.

When he arrived it was nearly dark. Mr. Pothecary was tired, dirty, battered, torn, outraged, bruised and hatless. And his spirit hardened. The forces of reaction surged through him. He was done with good actions. He felt vindictive, spiteful, wicked. Slowly he took the last turning and his eye once more alighted on—the Peels's fowl house.

And there came to him a vague desire to end his day by performing some action the contrary to good, something spiteful, petty, malign. His soul demanded some recompense for its abortive energies. And then he remembered that the Peels were away. They were returning late that evening. The two intensive fowl houses were at the end of the kitchen garden, where all the young spring cabbages and peas had just been planted. They could be approached between a slit in the narrow black fence adjacent to a turnip field. Rather a long way round. A simple and rather futile plan sprang into his mind, but he was too tired to think of anything more criminal or diabolic.

He would creep round to the back, get through the fence, force his way into the fowl-house. Then he would kick out all those expensive Rhode Island pampered hens and lock them out. Inside he would upset everything and smash the place to pieces. The fowls would get all over the place. They would eat the young vegetables. Some of them would get lost, stolen by gypsies, killed by rats. What did he care? The Peels would probably not discover the outrage till the morrow, and they would never know who did it. Edwin chuckled inwardly, and rolled his eyes like the smooth villain of a fit-up melodrama. He glanced up and down to see that no one was looking, then he got across a gate and entered the turnip field.

Within five minutes he was forcing the door of the fowl-house with a spade. The fowls were already settling down for the night, and they clucked rather alarmingly, but Edwin's blood was up. He chased them all out, forty-five of them, and made savage lunges at them with his feet. Then he upset all the com he could find, and poured water on it and jumped on it. He smashed the complicated invention suspended from the ceiling, whereby the fowls had to reach up and get one grain of com at a time. To his joy he found a pot of green paint, which he flung promiscuously over the walls and floor (and incidentally his clothes).

Then he crept out and bolted both of the doors.

The sleepy creatures were standing about outside, some feebly pecking about on the ground. He chased them through into the vegetable garden; then he rubbed some of the dirt and paint from his clothes and returned to the road.

When he arrived home he said to his wife:

"I fell off a tram on Waterloo Bridge. Lost my hat."

He was cold and wet and his teeth were chattering. His wife bustled him off to bed and gave him a little hot grog.

Between the sheets he recovered contentment. He gurgled exultantly at this last and only satisfying exploit of the day. He dreamed lazily of the blind rage of the Peels ....

It must have been half-past ten when his wife came up to bring him some hot gruel. He had been asleep. She put the cup by the bedside and rearranged his pillow.

"Feeling better?" she asked.

"Yes. I'm right," he murmured.

She sat on a chair by the side of the bed and after a few minutes remarked:

"You've missed an excitement while you've been asleep."

"Oh?"

Them Others

It is always disturbing to me when things fall into pattern form, when in fact incidents of real life dovetail with each other in such. a manner as to suggest the shape of a story. A story is a nice neat little thing with what is called a "working up" and a climax, and life is a clumsy, ungraspable thing, very incomplete in its periods, and with a poor sense of climax. In fact, death—which is a very uncertain quantity—is the only definite note it strikes, and even death has an uncomfortable way of setting other things in motion. If, therefore, in telling you about my friend Mrs. Ward, I am driven to the usual shifts of the story-teller, you must believe me that it is because this narrative concerns visions: Mrs. Ward's visions, my visions, and your visions. Consequently I am dependent upon my own poor powers of transcription to mold these visions into some sort of shape, and am driven into the position of a story-teller against my will. The first vision, then, concerns the back view of the Sheldrake Road, which, as you know, butts on to the railway embankment near Dalston Junction station. If you are of an adventurous turn of mind you shall accompany me, and we will creep up to the embankment together and look down into these back yards.

(We shall be liable to a fine of 40/-, according to a bye-law of the Railway Company, for doing so, but the experience will justify us.)

There are twenty-two of these small buff-brick houses huddled together in this road, and there is surely no more certain way of judging not only the character of the individual inhabitants, but of their mode of life, than by a survey of these somewhat pathetic yards. Is it not, for instance, easy to determine the timid, well ordered mind of little Miss Person, the dressmaker at number nine, by its garden of neat mud paths, with its thin patch of meager grass, and the small bed of skimpy geraniums? Cannot one read the tragedy of those dreadful Alleson people at number four? The garden is a wilderness of filth and broken bottles, where even the weeds seem chary of establishing themselves. In fact, if we listen carefully—and the trains are not making too much noise—we can hear the shrill crescendo of Mrs. Alleson's voice cursing at her husband in the kitchen, the half-empty gin bottle between them.

The methodical pushfulness and practicability of young Mr. and Mrs. Andrew MacFarlane is evident at number fourteen. They have actually grown a patch of potatoes, and some scarlet-runners, and there is a chicken run near the house.

Those irresponsible people, the O'Neals, have grown a bod of hollyhocks, but for the rest the garden is untidy and unkempt. One could almost swear they were connected in some obscure way with the theatrical profession.

Mrs. Abbot's garden is a sort of playground. It has asphalt paths, always swarming with small and not too clean children, and there are five lines of washing suspended above the mud. Every day seems to be Mrs. Abbot's washing day. Perhaps she "does" for others. Sam Abbot is certainly a lazy, insolent old rascal, and such always seem destined to be richly fertile. Mrs. Abbot is a pleasant "body," though. The Greens are the swells of the road. George Green is in the grocery line, and both his sons are earning good money, and one daughter has piano lessons. The narrow strip of yard is actually divided into two sections, a flower-garden and a kitchen-garden. And they are the only people who have flower-boxes in the front.

Number eight is a curious place. Old Mr. Bilge lives there. He spends most of his time in the garden, but nothing ever seems to come up. He stands about in his shirt-sleeves, and with a circular paper hat on his head, like a printer. They say he was formerly a com merchant but has lost all his money. He keeps the garden very neat and tidy, but nothing seems to grow. He stands there staring at the beds, as though he found their barrenness quite unaccountable.

Number eleven is unoccupied, and number twelve is Mrs. Ward's.

We now come to an important vision, and I want you to come down with me from the embankment and to view Mrs. Ward's garden from inside, and also Mrs. Ward as I saw her on that evening when I had occasion to pay my first visit.

It had been raining, but the sun had come out. We wandered round the paths together, and I can see her old face now, lined and seamed with years of anxious toil and struggle; her long, bony arms, slightly withered, but moving restlessly in the direction of snails and slugs.

"O dear! O dear!" she was saying. "What with the dogs, and the cats, and the snails, and the trains, it's wonderful anything comes up at all!"

Mrs. Ward's garden has a character of its own, and I cannot account for it. There is nothing very special growing—a few pansies and a narrow border of London Pride, several clumps of unrecognizable things that haven't flowered, the grass patch in only fair order, and at the end of the garden an unfinished rabbit hutch. But there is about Mrs. Ward's garden an atmosphere. There is something about it that reflects her placid eye, the calm, somewhat contemplative way she has of looking right through things, as though they didn't concern her too closely. As though, in fact, she were too occupied with her own inner visions.

"'Oh," she says in answer to my query, "we don't mind the trains at all. In fact, me and my Tom we often come out here and sit after supper. And Tom smokes his pipe. We like to hear the trains go by."

She gazes abstractedly at the embankment.

"I like to hear things ... going on and that. It's Dalston Junction a little further on. The trains go from there to all parts, right out into the country they do ... ever so far .... My Ernie went from Dais-ton."

She adds the last in a changed tone of voice. And now perhaps we come to the most important vision of all—Mrs. Ward's vision of "my Ernie."

I ought perhaps to mention that I had never met "my Ernie." I can only see him through Mrs. Ward's eyes. At the time when I met her, he had been away at the war for nearly a year. I need hardly say that "my Ernie" was a paragon of sons. He was brilliant, handsome, and incredibly clever. Everything that "my Ernie" said was treasured. Every opinion that he expressed stood. If "my Ernie" liked any one, that person was always a welcome guest. If "my Ernie" disliked any one they were not to be tolerated, however plausible they might appear.

I had seen Ernie's photograph, and I must confess that ho appeared a rather weak, extremely ordinary-looking young man, but then I would rather trust to Mrs. Ward's visions than the art of any photographer.

Tom Ward was a mild, ineffectual-looking old man, with something of Mrs. Ward's placidity but with nothing of her strong individual poise. He had some job in a gas-works. There was also a daughter named Lily, a brilliant person who served in a tea-shop, and sometimes went to theaters with young men. To both husband and daughter Mrs. Ward adopted an affectionate, mothering, almost pitying attitude. But with "my Ernie" it was quite a different thing. I can see her stooping figure, and her silver-white hair gleaming in the sun as we come to the unfinished rabbit-hutch, and the curious wistful tones of her voice as she touches it and says:

"When my Ernie comes home .... "

The war to her. was some unimaginable but disconcerting affair centered round Ernie. People seemed to have got into some desperate trouble, and Ernie was the only one capable of getting them out of it. I could not at that time gauge how much Mrs. Ward realized the dangers the boy was experiencing. She always spoke with conviction that he would return safely. Nearly every other sentence contained some reference to things that were to happen "when my Ernie comes home." What doubts and fears she had were only recognizable by the subtlest shades in her voice.

When we looked over the wall into the deserted garden next door, she said: "O dear! I'm afraid they'll never let that place. It's been empty since the Stellings went away. Oh, years ago, before this old war."

II

It was on the occasion of my second visit that Mrs. Ward told me more about the Stellings. It appeared that they were a German family, of all things! There was a Mr, Stelling, and a Mrs. Frow Stelling, and two boys.

Mr. Stelling was a watchmaker, and he came from a place called Bremen. It was a very sad story Mrs. Ward told me. They had only been over here for ten months when Mr. Stelling died, and Mrs. Prow Stelling and the boys went back to Germany.

During the time of the Stellings' sojourn in the Sheldrake Road it appeared that the Wards had seen quite a good deal of them, and though it would be an exaggeration to say that they ever became great friends, they certainly got through, that period without any unpleasantness, and even developed a certain degree of intimacy.

"Allowing for their being foreigners," Mrs. Ward explained, "they were quite pleasant people."
On one or two occasions they invited each other to supper, and I wish my visions were sufficiently clear to envisage those two families indulging this social habit.

According to Mrs. Ward, Mr. Stelling was a kind little man with a round fat face. He spoke English fluently, but Mrs. Ward objected to his table manners.

"When my Tom eats," she said, "you don't hear a sound—I look after that!

But that Mr. Stelling ... O dear!"

The trouble with Mrs. Stelling was that she could only speak a few words of English, but Mrs. Ward said "she was a pleasant enough little body," and she established herself quite definitely in Mrs. Ward's affections for the reason that she was so obviously and so passionately devoted to her two sons.

"Oh, my word, though, they do have funny ways—these foreigners," she continued. "The things they used to eat! most peculiar! I've known them eat stewed prunes with hot meat!"

Mrs. Ward repeated, "Stewed prunes with hot meat!" several times, and shook her head, as though this exotic mixture was a thing to be sternly discouraged. But she acknowledged that Mrs. Prow Stelling was in some ways a very good cook, in fact, her cakes were really wonderful, "the sort of thing you can't even buy in a shop."

About the boys there seemed to be a little divergence of opinion. They were both also fat-faced, and their heads were "almost shaved like convicts." The elder one wore spectacles and was rather noisy, but:

"My Ernie liked the younger one. Oh, yes, my Ernie said that young Hans was quite a nice boy. It was funny the way they spoke, funny and difficult to understand."

It was very patent that between the elder boy and Ernie, who were of about the same age, there was an element of rivalry which was perhaps more accentuated in the attitude of the mothers than in the boys themselves. Mrs. Ward could find little virtue in this elder boy. Most of her criticism of the family was leveled against him. The rest she found only a little peculiar. She said she had never heard such a funny Christian name as Prow. Florrie she had heard of, and even Flora, but not Frow. I suggested that perhaps Frow might be some sort of title, but she shook her head and said that that was what she was always known as in the Sheldrake Road, "Mrs. Frow Stelling."

In spite of Mrs. Ward's lack of opportunity for greater intimacy on account of the language problem, her own fine imaginative qualities helped her a great deal. And in one particular she seemed curiously vivid. She gathered an account from one of them—I'm not sure whether it was Mr. or Mrs. Frow Stelling or one of the boys—of a place they described near their home in Bremen. There was a narrow street of high buildings by a canal, and a little bridge that led over into a gentleman's park. At a point where the canal turned sharply eastwards there was a clump of linden-trees, where one could go in the summer-time, and under their shade one might sit and drink light beer, and listen to a band that played in the early part of the evening.

Mrs. Ward was curiously clear about that. She said she often thought about Mr. Stelling sitting there after his day's work. It must have been very pleasant for him, and he seemed to miss this luxury in Dalston more than anything. Once Ernie, in a friendly mood, had taken him into the four-ale bar of "The Unicorn" at the corner of the Sheldrake Road, but Mr. Stelling did not seem happy. Ernie acknowledged afterwards that it had been an unfortunate evening. The bar had been rather crowded, and there was a man and two women who had all been drinking too much. In any case, Mr. Stelling had been obviously restless there, and he had said afterwards:

"It is not that one wishes to drink only ... ", And he had shaken his fat little head, and had never been known to visit "The Unicorn" again.

Mr. Stelling died quite suddenly of some heart trouble, and Mrs. Ward could not get it out of her head that his last illness was brought about by his disappointment and grief in not being able to go and sit quietly under the linden trees after his day's work and listen to a band.

"You know, my dear," she said, "when you get accustomed to a thing, it's had for you to leave it off." When poor Mr. Stelling died, Mrs. Frow Stelling was heart-broken, and I have reason to believe that Mrs. Ward went in and wept with her, and in their dumb way they forged the chains of some desperate understanding. When Mrs. Frow Stelling went back to Germany they promised to write to each other. But they never did, and for a very good reason. As Mrs. Ward said, she was "no scholard," and as for Mrs. Frow Stelling, her English was such a doubtful quantity, she probably never got beyond addressing the envelope.

"That was three years ago," said Mrs. Ward. "Them boys must be eighteen and nineteen now."

If I have intruded too greatly into the intimacy of Mrs. Ward's life, one of my excuses must be—not that I am "a scholard" but that I am in any case able to read a simple English letter. I was in fact on several occasions "requisitioned." When Lily was not at home, sonic one had to read Ernie's letters out loud. The arrival of Ernie's letters was always an inspiring experience. I should perhaps be in the garden with Mrs. Ward, when Tom would come hurrying out to the back, and call out:

"Mother! a letter from Ernie!"

And then there would be such excitement and commotion. The first thing was always the hunt for Mrs. Ward's spectacles. They were never where she had put them. Tom would keep on turning the letter over in his hands, and examining the postmark, and he would reiterate:

"Well, what did you do with them, mother?"

At length they would be found in some unlikely place, and she would take the letter tremblingly to the light. I never knew quite how much Mrs. Ward could read. She could certainly read a certain amount. I saw her old eyes sparkling and her tongue moving jerkily between her parted lips, as though she were formulating the words she read, and she would keep on repeating:

"T'ch! T'ch! O dear, O dear, the things he says!"

And Tom impatiently by the door would say:

"Well, what does he say?"

She never attempted to read the letter out loud, but at last she would wipe her spectacles and say:

"Oh, you read it, sir. The things he says!"

They were indeed very good letters of Ernie's, written apparently in the highest spirits. There was never a grumble, not a word. One might gather that he was away with a lot of young bloods on some sporting expedition, in which football, rags, sing-songs, and strange feeds played a conspicuous part. I read a good many of Ernie's letters, and I do not remember that he ever made a single reference to the horrors of war, or said anything about his own personal discomforts. The boy must have had something of his mother in him in spite of the photograph.

And between the kitchen and the yard Mrs. "Ward would spend her day placidly content, for Ernie never failed to write. There was sometimes a lapse of a few days, but the letter seldom failed to come every fortnight.

It would be difficult to know what Mrs. Ward's actual conception of the war was. She never read the newspapers, for the reason, as she explained, that "there was nothing in them these days except about this old war." She occasionally dived into Reynold's newspaper on Sundays to see if there were any interesting law cases or any news of a romantic character. There was nothing romantic in the war news. It was all preposterous. She did indeed read the papers for the first few weeks, but this was for the reason that she had some vague idea that they might contain some account of Ernie's doings. But as they did not, she dismissed them with contempt.

But I found her one night in a peculiarly preoccupied mood. She was out in the garden, and she kept staring abstractedly over the fence into the unoccupied ground next door. It appeared that it had dawned upon her that the war was to do with "these Germans," that in fact we were fighting the Germans, and then she thought of the Stellings. Those boys would now be about eighteen and nineteen. They would be fighting too. They would be fighting against Ernie. This seemed very peculiar.

"Of course," she said, "I never took to that elder boy—a greedy rough sort of boy he was. But I'm sure my Ernie wouldn't hurt young Hans."

She meditated for a moment as though she were contemplating what particular action Ernie would take in the matter. She knew he didn't like the elder boy but she doubted whether he would want to do anything very violent to him.

"They went out to a music-hall one night together," she explained, as though a friendship cemented in this luxurious fashion could hardly be broken by an unreasonable display of passion.

It was a few weeks later that the terror suddenly crept into Mrs. Ward's life. Ernie's letters ceased abruptly. The fortnight passed, then three weeks, four weeks, five weeks, and not a word. I don't think that Mrs. Ward's character at any time stood out so vividly as during those weeks of stress. It is true she appeared a little feebler, and she trembled in her movements, whilst her eyes seemed abstracted as though all the power in them were concentrated in her ears, alert for the bell or the knock. She started visibly at odd moments, and her imagination was always carrying her tempestuously to the front door only to answer—a milkman or a casual hawker. But she never expressed her fear in words. When Tom came home—he seemed to have aged rapidly—he would come bustling out into the garden, and cry tremblingly:

"There ain't been no letter to-day, mother?" And she would say quite placidly:

"No, not to-day, Tom. It'll come to-morrow, I expect."

And she would rally him and talk of little things, and get busy with his supper. And in the garden I would try and talk to her about her clump of pansies, and the latest yam about the neighbors, and I tried to get between her and the rabbit hutch with its dumb appeal of incompletion. And I would notice her staring curiously over into the empty garden next door, as though she were being assailed by some disturbing apprehensions. Ernie would not hurt that eldest boy ... but suppose ... if things were reversed ... there was something inexplicable and terrible lurking in this passive silence.

During this period the old man was suddenly taken very ill. He came home one night with a high temperature and developed pneumonia. He was laid up for many weeks, and she kept back the telegram that came while he was almost unconscious, and she tended him night and day, nursing her own anguish with a calm face.

For the telegram told her that her Ernie was "missing, believed wounded."

I do not know at what period she told the father this news, but it was certainly not till he was convalescent. And the old man seemed to sink into a kind of apathy. He sat feebly in front of the kitchen fire, coughing and making no effort to control his grief.

Outside the great trains went rushing by, night and day. Things were "going on," but they were all meaningless, cruel.

We made enquiries at the War Office, but they could not amplify the laconic telegram.

And then the winter came on, and the gardens were bleak in the Sheldrake Road. And Lily ran away and married a young tobacconist, who was earning twenty-five shillings a week. And old Tom was dismissed from the gas-works. His work was not proving satisfactory. And he sat about at home and moped. And in the meantime the price of foodstuffs was going up, and coals were a luxury. And so in the early morning Mrs. Ward would go off and work for Mrs. Abbot at the wash-tub, and she would earn eight or twelve shillings a week.

It is difficult to know how they managed during those days, but one could see that Mrs. Ward was buoyed up by some poignant hope. She would not give way. Eventually old Tom did get some work to do at a stationer's. The work was comparatively light, and the pay equally so, so Mrs. Ward still continued to work for Mrs. Abbot.

My next vision of Mrs. Ward concerns a certain winter evening. I could not see inside the kitchen, but the old man could be heard complaining. His querulous voice was rambling on, and Mrs. Ward was standing by the door leading into the garden. She had returned from her day's work and was scraping a pan out into a bin near the door. A train shrieked by, and the wind was blowing a fine rain against the house. Suddenly she stood up and looked up at the sky; then she pushed back her hair from her brow, and frowned at the dark house next door. Then she turned and said:

"Oh, I don't know, Tom, if we've got to do it, we must do it. If them others can stand it, we can stand it. Whatever them others can do, we can do."

And then my visions jump rather wildly. And the war becomes to me epitomized in two women. One in this dim doorway in our obscure suburb of Dalston, scraping out a pan, and the other perhaps in some dark high house near a canal on the outskirts of Bremen. Them others! These two women silently enduring. And the trains rushing by, and all the dark, mysterious forces of the night operating on them equivocally.

Poor Mrs. Frow Stelling! Perhaps those boys of hers are "missing, believed killed." Perhaps they are killed for certain.! She is as much outside "the things going on" as Mrs. Ward. Perhaps she is equally as patient, as brave.

And Mrs. Ward enters the kitchen, and her eyes are blazing with a strange light as she says:

"We'll hear to-morrow, Tom. And if we don't hear to-morrow, we'll hear the next day. And if we don't hear the next day, we'll hear the day after. And if we don't ... if we don't never hear ... again ... if them others can stand it, we can stand it, I say."

And then her voice breaks, and she cries a little, for endurance has its limitations, and—the work is hard at Mrs. Abbot's.

And the months go by, and she stoops a little more as she walks, and—some one has thrown a cloth over the rabbit-hutch with its unfinished roof. And Mrs. Ward is curiously retrospective. It is useless to tell her of the things of the active world. She listens politely but she does not hear. She is full of reminiscences of Ernie's and Lily's childhood. She recounts again and again the story of how Ernie when he was a little boy ordered five tons of coal from a coal merchant to be sent to a girls' school in Dalston High Road. She describes the coal carts arriving in the morning, and the consternation of the head-mistress.

"O dear, O dear," she says; "the things he did!"

She does not talk much of the Stellings, but one day she says meditatively: "Mrs. Frow Stelling thought a lot of that boy Hans. So she did of the other, as far as that goes. It's only natural like, I suppose."

As time went on Tom Ward lost all hope. He said he was convinced that the boy was killed. Having arrived at this conclusion he seemed to become more composed. He gradually began to accustom himself to the new point of view. But with Mrs. Ward the exact opposite was the case. She was convinced that the boy was alive, but she suffered terribly.

There came a time—it was in early April—when one felt that the strain could not last. She seemed to lose all interest in the passing world and lived entirely within herself. Even the arrival of Lily's baby did not rouse her. She looked at the child queerly, as though she doubted whether any useful or happy purpose was served by its appearance.

It was a boy.

In spite of her averred optimism she lost her tremulous sense of apprehension when the bell went or the front door was tapped. She let the milkman—and even the postman—wait.

When she spoke it was invariably of things that happened years ago. Sometimes she talked about the Stellings, and on one Sunday she made a strange pilgrimage out to Finchley and visited Mr. Stelling's grave. I don't know what she did there, but she returned looking very exhausted and unwell. As a matter of fact, she was unwell for some days after this visit, and she suffered violent twinges of rheumatism in her legs.

I now come to my most unforgettable vision of Mrs. Ward.

It was a day at the end of April, and warm for the time of year. I was standing in the garden with her and it was nearly dark. A goods train had been shunting, and making a great deal of noise in front of the house, and at last had disappeared. I had not been able to help noticing that Mrs. Ward's garden was curiously neglected for her for the time of year. The grass was growing on the paths, and the snails had left their silver trail over all the fences.

I was telling her a rumor I had heard about the railway porter and his wife at number twenty-three, and she seemed fairly interested, for she had known John Hemsley, the porter, fifteen years ago when Ernie was a baby. There were two old broken Windsor chairs out in the garden, and on one was a zinc basin in which were some potatoes. She was peeling them, as Lily and her husband were coming to supper. By the kitchen door was a small sink. When she had finished the potatoes, she stood up and began to pour the water down the sink, taking care not to let the skins go too. I was noticing her old bent back, and her long bony hands gripping the sides of the basin, when suddenly a figure came limping round the bend of the house from the side passage, and two arms were thrown round her waist, and a voice said:

"Mind them skins don't go down the sink, mother. They'll stop it up!"

VI

As I explained to Ernie afterwards, it was an extremely foolish thing to do. If his mother had had anything wrong with her heart, it might have been very serious. There have been many cases of people dying from the shock of such an experience.

As it was, she merely dropped the basin and stood there trembling like a leaf, and Ernie laughed loud and uproariously. It must have been three or four minutes before she could regain her speech, and then all she could manage to say was:

"Ernie! ... My Ernie!"

And the boy laughed, and ragged his mother, and pulled her into the house, and Tom appeared and stared at his son, and said feebly:

"Well, I never!"

I don't know how it was that I found myself intruding upon the sanctity of the inner life of the Ward family that evening. I had never had a meal there before, but I felt that I was holding a sort of watching brief over the soul and body of Mrs. Ward. I had a little medical training in my early youth, and this may have been one of the reasons which prompted me to stay.

When Lily and her husband appeared we sat down to a meal of mashed potatoes and onions stewed in milk, with bread and cheese, and very excellent it was.

Lily and her husband took the whole thing in a boisterous, high comedy manner that fitted in with the mood of Ernie. Old Tom sat there staring at his son, and repeating at intervals:

"Well, I never!"

And Mrs. Ward hovered round the boy's plate. Her eyes divided their time between his plate and his face, and she hardly spoke all the evening.

Ernie's story was remarkable enough. He told it disconnectedly and rather incoherently. There were moments when he rambled in a rather peculiar way, and sometimes he stammered, and seemed unable to frame a sentence. Lily's husband went out to fetch some beer to celebrate the joyful occasion, and Ernie drank his in little sips, and spluttered. The boy must have suffered considerably, and he had a wound in the abdomen, and another in the right forearm which for a time had paralyzed him.

As far as I could gather, his story was this:

He and a platoon of men had been ambushed and had had to surrender. When being sent back to a base, three of them tried to escape from the train, which had been held up at night. He did not know what had happened to the other two men, but it was on this occasion that he received his abdominal wound at the hands of a guard.

He had then been sent to some infirmary where he was fairly well treated, but as soon as his wound had healed a little, he had been suddenly sent to some fortress prison, presumably as a punishment.

He hadn't the faintest idea how long he had been confined there. He said it seemed like fifteen years. It was probably nine months. He had solitary confinement in a cell, which was like a small lavatory. He had fifteen minutes' exercise every day in a yard with some other prisoners, who were Russians he thought. He spoke to no one. He used to sing and recite in his cell, and there were times when he was quite convinced that he was "off his chump." He said he had lost "all sense of everything" when he was suddenly transferred to another prison. Here the conditions were somewhat better and he was made to work. He said he wrote six or seven letters home from there, but received no reply. The letters certainly never reached Dalston. The food was execrable, but a big improvement on the dungeon. He was only there a few weeks when he and some thirty other prisoners were sent suddenly to work on the land at a kind of settlement. He said that the life there would have been tolerable if it hadn't been for the fact that the Commandant was an absolute brute. The food was worse than in the prison, and they were punished severely for the most trivial offenses.

It was here, however, that he met a sailor named Martin, a Royal Naval reservist, an elderly thickset man with a black beard and only one eye. Ernie said that this Martin "was an artist. He wangled everything. He had a genius for getting what he wanted. He would get a beef-steak out of stone." In fact, it was obvious that the whole of Ernie's narrative was colored by his vision of Martin. He said he'd never met such a chap in his life. He admired him enormously, and he was also a little afraid of him.

By some miraculous means peculiar to sailors, Martin acquired a compass. Ernie hardly knew what a compass was, but the sailor explained to him that it was all that was necessary to take you straight to England. Ernie said he "had had enough escaping. It didn't agree with his health," but so strong was his faith and belief in Martin that he ultimately agreed to try with him.

He said Martin's method of escape was the coolest thing he'd ever seen. He planned it all beforehand. It was the fag-end of the day, and the whistle had gone and the prisoners were trooping back across a potato-field. Martin and Ernie were very slow. They lingered apparently to discuss some matter connected with the soil. There were two sentries in sight, one near them and the other perhaps a hundred yards away. The potato field was on a slope and at the bottom of the field were two lines of barbed wire entanglements. The other prisoners passed out of sight, and the sentry near them called out something, probably telling them to hurry up. They started to go up the field when suddenly Martin staggered and clutched his throat. Then he fell over backwards and commenced to have an epileptic fit. Ernie said it was the realest thing he'd ever seen. The sentry ran up, at the same time whistling to his comrade. Ernie released Martin's collar-band and tried to help him. Both the sentries approached, and Ernie stood back. He saw them bending over the prostrate man, when suddenly a most extraordinary thing happened. Both their heads were brought together with fearful violence. One fell completely senseless, but the other staggered forward and groped for his rifle.

When Ernie told this part of the story he kept dabbing his forehead with his handkerchief.

"I never seen such a man as Martin I don't think," he said. "Lord! He had a fist like a leg of mutton. He laid 'em out neatly on the grass, took off their coats and most of their other clothes, and flung 'em over the barbed wire and then swarmed over like a cat. I had more difficulty, but he got me across too, somehow. Then we carted the clothes away to the next line.

"We got up into a wood that night, and Martin draws out his compass and he says: 'We've got a hundred and seven miles to do in night shifts, cully. And if we make a slip we're shot as safe as knife.' It sounded the maddest scheme in the world, but I somehow felt that Martin would get through it. The only thing that saved me was that—that I didn't have to think. I simply left everything to him. If I'd started thinking I could have gone mad. I had it fixed in my mind,' either he does it or he doesn't do it. I can't help it.' I reely don't remember much about that journey. It was all a dream like. We did all our travelin' at night by compass, and hid by day. Neither of us had a word of German. But Gawd's truth! that man Martin was a marvel! He turned our trousers inside out, and made 'em look like ordinary laborers' trousers. He disappeared the first night and came back with some other old clothes. We lived mostly on raw potatoes we dug out of the ground with our hands, but not always.

One night he came back with a fowl which he cooked in a hole in the earth, making a fire with a flint and some dry stuff he pinched from a farm. I believed Martin could have stole an egg from under a hen without her noticing it. He was the coolest card there ever was. Of course there was a lot of trouble one way and another. It wasn't always easy to find wooded country or protection of any sort. We often ran into people and they stared at us, and we shifted our course. But I think we were only addressed three or four times by men, and then Martin's methods were the simplest in the world. He just looked sort of blank for a moment, and then knocked them clean out, and bolted. Of course they were after us all the time, and it was this constant tacking and shifting ground that took so long. Fancy! he never had a map, you know, nothing but the compass.

We didn't know what sort of country we were coming to, nothing. We just crept through the night like cats.

I believe Martin could see in the dark He killed a dog one night with his hands .... It was necessary."

VII

It was impossible to discover from Ernie how long this amazing journey lasted—the best part of two months I believe. He was himself a little uncertain with regard to many incidents, whether they were true or whether they were hallucinations. He suffered greatly from his wound and had periods of feverish ness. But one morning, he said, Martin began "prancing." He seemed to develop some curious sense that they were near the Dutch frontier. And then, according to Ernie, "a cat wasn't in it with Martin."

He was very mysterious about the actual crossing. I gathered that there had been some "clumsy" work with sentries. It was at that time that Ernie got a bullet through his arm. When he got to Holland he was very ill. It was not that the wound was a very serious one, but, as he explained:

"Me blood was in a bad state. I was nearly down and out."

He was very kindly treated by some Dutch Sisters in a convent hospital. But he was delirious for a long time, and when he became more normal they wanted to communicate with his people in England, but this didn't appeal to the dramatic sense of Ernie.

"I thought I'd spring a surprise packet on you," he said, grinning.

We asked about Martin, but Ernie said he never saw him again. He went away while Ernie was delirious, and they said he had gone to Rotterdam to take ship somewhere. He thought Holland was a dull place.

During the relation of this narrative my attention was divided between watching the face of Ernie and the face of Ernie's mother.

I am quite convinced that she did not listen to the story at all. She never took her eyes from his face, and although her tongue was following the flow of his remarks, her mind was occupied with the vision of Ernie when he was a little boy, and when he ordered five tons of coal to be sent to the girls' school.

When he had finished she said:

"Did you meet either of them young Stellings?"

And Ernie laughed rather uproariously and said no, he didn't have the pleasure of renewing their acquaintance.

On his way home, it appeared, he had reported himself at headquarters, and his discharge was inevitable.

"So now you'll be able to finish the rabbit-hutch," said Lily's husband, and we all laughed again, with the exception of Mrs. Ward.

I found her later standing alone in the garden. It was a warm Spring night. There was no moon, but the sky appeared restless with its burden of trembling stars. She had an old shawl drawn round her shoulders, and she stood there very silently, with her arms crossed.

"Well, this is splendid news, Mrs. Ward," I said.

She started a little, and coughed, and pulled the shawl closer round her. She said, "Yes, sir," very faintly.

I don't think she was very conscious of me. She still appeared immersed in the contemplation of her inner visions. Her eyes settled upon the empty house next door, and I thought I detected the trail of a tear glistening on her checks. I lighted my pipe. We could hear Ernie, and Lily, and Lily's husband still laughing and talking inside.

"She used to make a very good puddin'," Mrs. Ward said suddenly, at random. "Dried fruit inside, and that. My Ernie liked it very much ... "

Somewhere away in the distance—probably outside "The Unicorn"—some one was playing a comet. A train crashed by and disappeared, leaving a trail of foul smoke which obscured the sky. The smoke cleared slowly away. I struck another match to light my pipe.

It was quite true. On either side of her cheek a tear had trickled. She was trembling a little, worn out by the emotions of the evening.

There was a moment of silence, unusual for Dalston. "It's all very ... perplexin' and that," she said quietly.

And then I knew for certain that in that great hour of her happiness her mind was assailed by strange and tremulous doubts. She was thinking of "them others" a little wistfully. She was doubting whether one could rejoice—when the thing became clear and actual to one—without sending out one's thoughts into the dark garden to "them others" who were suffering too. And she had come out into this little meager yard at Dalston and had gazed through the mist and smoke upwards to the stars, because she wanted peace intensely, and so she sought it within herself, because she knew that real peace is a thing which concerns the heart alone.

And so I left her standing there, and I went my way, for I knew that she was wiser than I.

The call was irresistible. I had tramped for nearly two hours along the white road, when suddenly a long stretch of open heath with sparsely-scattered trees and high gorse bushes invited me to break my journey and to seek the shade of a wood that fringed it on the western side. The ground sloped upwards at a steep gradient and I was soon among the cool shadows of the larch trees. After climbing for nearly half-an-hour I found myself on a kind of plateau, looking down upon one of the most beautiful sights in the world, the Weald of Sussex trembling in a gray heat mist framed through a thin belt of trees. I pushed forward, determining to rest in this most attractive spot.

Nearing the fringe of this little clump, I observed a bent tree in a clearing. As I approached it it occurred to me that the subject before me was curiously like Corot's famous masterpiece. It was indeed a wonderful and romantic spot. Beneath me a river rambled through the meadows and became lost in the gray-line distances. There was no sign of civilization except sleepy cattle and the well-kept fields, and occasionally a village nestling in the hollow of the downs. The only sound was the movement of leaves, the drone of bees and the lowing of cattle in the distant meadows.

I sat down on the bent tree, and as I looked around it occurred to me that the spot I had chosen was like a little arbor. It might have been the home of some God of ancient Britain, who could have lived here undisturbed through all the generations. I was wondering whether any one else had ever penetrated to this glorious retreat from the world when my eye caught a small square of white paper pinned on the trunk of the bent tree, I examined it, and lo! on it was written in ink: "Gone to lunch. Back in 20 Minutes."

Now if there is one thing that makes me wretchedly unhappy it is the action of people who find pleasure in disfiguring nature, in carving their initials on tree trunks, in scattering paper and orange-peel about the country-side; but somehow, when I caught sight of this absurd city office formula pinned to a tree in this most inaccessible and romantic spot, I must confess that "my lungs did crow like Chanticleer." I felt that here indeed was the work of a vast and subtle humorist. The formula was so familiar. How often had I waited hours in murky passages, buoyed up by this engaging promise! It seemed so redolent of drab staircases, and files and roll-top desks, that its very mention out here struck a fantastic note. That any one should suggest that he carried on a business here, that his time was precious, that after gulping down a cup of coffee, he would rush back, cope with increasing press of affairs, seemed to me wonderfully and amazingly funny. I must acknowledge that I made myself rather ridiculous. I laughed till the tears streamed down my face, and my only desire was for a companion with whom to share the manna of this gigantic jest. I looked at the card again. It was comparatively clean, so I presumed that the joke had been perpetrated quite recently.

And then I began to wonder whether the jester would return, whether, after all, the slip had any significance. Was it the message of a poacher to a friend? Or was this the secret meeting place of some gods of High Finance? I determined in any case to wait the allotted span, and in the meantime I stretched myself on the stem of the bent tree, and, lighting a cigarette, prepared to enjoy the tranquillity of the scene.

It was barely ten minutes before my siesta was disturbed by a man coming stealthily up the slope. He was a medium-sized, sallow-faced fellow with small tired eyes set in dark hollows. He was wearing a tail-coat and a bowler hat. He shuffled quickly through the wood, pushing the branches of the trees away from him. His eyes fixed me furtively, and as he entered the little arbor, he took off his hat and fidgeted with it, as though looking for a customary hook on which to hang it.

"I hope I haven't kept you waiting?" was his greeting.

"Not at all," I found myself answering, for lack of a more suitable reply. "Did Binders send you?" he asked tentatively.

"No," I replied, pulling myself together. "I just happened to come here."

A look of disappointment passed over his face. "Oh!" he said, walking up and down. "I sometimes do a bit with Binders and his friends, you know"—he waved his arms vaguely—"you know, from Corlesham."

Corlesham I knew to be a village rather more than two miles away, a sleepy hamlet of less than fifty souls.

"Oh, I see," I replied, more with the idea of not discouraging him than because any particular light had come to me.

He looked at me searchingly for some moments, and then, going over to a thick gorse-bush, he knelt down and grouped underneath and presently produced a thick pile of papers and circulars.

"I wonder whether you would like to do anything in these? These West Australians are good. They're right down to 65. If you can hold on, a sure thing. If you would like a couple of thousand now ..." he was nervously biting his nails; then he said, "Could you spare me a cigarette?"

I produced my case and handed him one.

"Thanks very much," he said. "They don't like me to smoke at home," and he waved his hand towards the north. I followed the direction, and just caught sight of the top of a gable of a large red-brick building through the trees.

So this was the solution!

"This is a glorious place," I said.

This seemed a very harmless platitude and one not likely to drive a being to despair. But it had a strange effect on my individual, for he sat down on a broken branch and burst into a paroxysm of invective.

"Oh, Gawd!" he said. "I hate it, hate the sight of it! Day after day—all the same! All these blinkin' trees and fields—all the same, nothing happenin' ever."

I found it very difficult to meet this outburst. I could think of nothing to say, so I kept silent. After a time he got up, puffing feverishly at the cigarette, and walked round the little arbor. Every now and then he would stop and make a gesture towards the shrubs. I believe he was visualizing files and folios, ledgers, and typewriters. He made a movement of opening and shutting drawers.

"You've been a bit run down, haven't you?" I said at last, with a feeble attempt to bridge the gulf. He looked at me uncertainly, and wiped the perspiration from his brow.

"I was unlucky," he said sullenly. "I worked like a nigger for thirty years, but so do the others—lots of them—and they're all right. Just sheer bad luck, if you know what I mean. I can do it now when they let me. That's why I come here. Binders helps me a bit. He sends me people. And, do you know?" he whispered to me confidentially, "I've got the postman on my side. He delivers me letters here at twopence a time. Look! here is my mail-box!" He stooped down and lifted a large stone and produced a further pile of correspondence and circulars. "Would you like to buy some of these Trinidads? I could work it for you."

He looked at me anxiously, and I made some elaborate excuse for not seizing such a splendid opportunity.

He sighed, and placed the papers back under the stone. "Have you ever dealt in big things?" he asked.

"I'm afraid not—in your sense," I answered, nurturing an instinctive sense of outraged superiority against this person who I felt despised me.

"You know what I mean by big things," he said fiercely. "Millions and millions, and the lives and works of millions of people! Do you know why I come down here to this rotten little clearing? Because it sometimes reminds me of my office off Throgmorton Street. Look! It was just this size. I had my desk over there. Horswall, my secretary, had his desk here. Here was the fireplace. The press just here by the window. Here the shelves with all the files. Can you imagine what it's like to have been there all those years, to have worked up what I did—all out of nothing, mark you!—to have got the whole rubber market in the hollow of my hand!—and then, oh, God! to be condemned to—this!" and he made a gesture of fierce contempt towards the Weald of Sussex.

"For nearly two years now," he continued, "I've been living in this hole."

"Nature has a way," I said, in my most sententious manner, "of coming back on us."

"Nayoher! Naycher!" he almost screamed. "Don't talk to me about Naycher! What sort of friend is Naycher to me or you? Naycher gives you inclinations, and then breaks you for following them! Two men fall into a pond—what does Naycher care that one man was trying to drown his enemy while the other was trying to save a dog? They both stand their chance of death. Naycher leads you up blind alleys and into marshes and lets you rot. Besides, isn't man Naycher? Isn't it Naycher for me to work and make money, as it is for these blighting birds to sing? Aren't roll-top desks as much Naycher as—these blasted trees? "

He blinked savagely at the surrounding scene. The smoke from a distant hamlet drifted sleepily heavenwards, like incense to the gods of the Downs.

"My father was a turner in Walham Green, and he apprenticed me to the joinery, but I had my ambitions even in those times." He nodded knowingly, and mopped his brow. "At eighteen I was a clerk in a wholesale house in St. Paul's Churchyard. For three years I worked there underground, by artificial light. Then I got made sub-manager of a wharf at the South end of Lower Thames Street. I was there for five years, and saved nearly three hundred pounds out of a salary of £120 a year. Then I met Jettison, and we started that office together, Jettison & Gateshead, Commission Agents. Work and struggle, work and struggle, year after year. But it was not till I got on to rubber that I began to make things move. That was eight years after. Do you remember the boom? I got in with Gayo, who had lived out in the Malay Straits—Knew everything—we got the whole game at our fingers' ends.

We knew just when to buy and just when to sell. Do you know, I've made as much as four thousand pounds in one afternoon, just talking on the telephone! And we done it all in that little room"- he gazed jealously round the little arbor in the hills, and scowled at me. Then he produced a packet of cigarettes and lighted one from the stump of the last.

"In those days, through Gayo's friends, we followed the whole course of the raw stuff. Then Gayo went out to Malay, and he used to cable me every few days, putting me on to the right thing. My God, he was a man! It went on for two years, when suddenly a cable came to say he was dead—fever, or something, up country. That was the end. The slump came soon after. I worked hard, but I never got control back. Down and down and down they went, as though Gayo was dragging them through the earth." His lower lip trembled as he rolled the emaciated cigarette over.

"Lord, what a fight I had, though I sat in that office there, in my shirt-sleeves, day and night for months on end, checking tapes, cabling, lying, faking, bluffing"—he chuckled with a meditative intensity. "I'd have done it then, if they'd given me time. But they closed in; there were two Scotch firms, and a man named Klaus. I knew they meant to do me down. There was a set against me. I wasn't there in the end. I was sitting in the office one night ...." He passed his hand over his brow and swept away a wasp that had settled there. He sat silent for some moments, as though trying to recall things, and twice started to speak without framing a sentence.

"My brother was very good to me," he said suddenly, waving his hand toward the red-brick gable in the trees. "He was very good to me all through." Then he added, with a sort of contemptuous shrug, "In the cabinet-making he was; got a little works at Bow—made about four hundred a year—married, and five children."

He sat for some minutes with his head in his hands, and then he sat up and gazed upon the joyous landscape with unseeing eyes.

I ventured to remark, "Well, I'm sure this place ought to do you good." He turned his melancholy eyes upon me, and sighed.

"Yes," he said, after a pause. "You're just the sort. I've seen so many of you about. Some of you have butterfly nets." He kept repeating at intervals, "Butterfly nets!" One felt that the last word in contumely had been uttered. He sank into an apathy of indifference. Then he broke out again.

"I tell you," he uttered fiercely, "that I had millions and millions. I controlled the work and the lives of millions of men, and you come here and talk to me of Naycher. Look at these damned trees! They go green in the summer, yellow in the autumn, and bare in the winter. Year after year, exactly the same thing, and that's all there is to it. I'm sick of the sight of them. But look at men! Think of their lives, the change and variety! What they can do! Their clothes, their furniture, their houses, their cities! Think of their power! The power of making and marring!"

"You mean the power of buying and selling," I ventured.

"Yes, that's just it!" he said, feeling that he was converting me.

"The power of buying and selling! Of making men rich or poor!" He stood up and waved his thin arms and gazed wildly round him. "Not chasing butterflies!"

At that moment we both became aware that a third person was on the scene. He was a well set-up man, with broad shoulders and narrow hips. He was dressed in a dark-blue serge suit and a tweed cap. He stepped quietly through the trees, and went up to my companion, and said:

"Ah! there you are, Mr. Gateshead. I'm afraid it's almost time for your afternoon nap, sir." And then, turning to me, he nodded and remarked: "A warm afternoon, sir!" He spoke with a quiet, suave voice that somehow conveyed the feeling of the "iron hand in the velvet glove." His voice seemed to have a sedative effect on Mr. Gateshead. My companion did not look at him, but he seemed to shrink within himself. A certain flush that had accompanied his excitement vanished, and his face looked old and set. He drew his narrow shoulders together and his figure bent. He stood abstractedly for a few moments, gazing at the trees around him, and then, with a vague gesture that was characteristic of him, he clutched the lapels of his coat, and with his head bent forward he walked away towards the building. He did not cast a glance in my direction, and the man in the serge suit nodded to me and followed him leisurely.

I clambered down the slope of the wood, and for some reason felt happy to get once more upon the road.

About half a mile from Corlesham I met the postman coming up the hill, wheeling his bicycle. He was a sandy-haired man, splendidly Saxon, with gray blue eyes and broad mouth. I asked him if there was a footpath to Corlesham, and he directed me.

"Do you have a long round?" I asked.

"Three or four mile, maybe," he said, looking at me narrowly. "It's a good pull up to the Institution," I ventured.

"What institution might that be?" he said, and his mild blue eyes disarmed me with their ingenuousness.

"The house with the three red gables," I answered.

"Oh!" came the reply. "You mean old Gateshead's."

"Does he own it?" I said incredulously.

"Ay, and he could own six others for all the difference it would make to his money. He owns half the county."

"And yet what a strange idea," I murmured insinuatingly." To own a large house and yet to have one's letters delivered in a wood!"

The postman swung his bag into a more comfortable position and looked across his machine at me with a grin.

"Those as has money can afford to have any ideas they like," he said at last. "I'm afraid his money doesn't make him very happy," I ventured, still groping for further enlightenment.

The postman gave his right pedal a vigorous twirl as a hint of departure. He then took out a packet of Navy Duty cigarettes and lighted one. This action seemed to stimulate his mental activities, and he leant on the handle-bars and said:

"Ay, if one has no money maybe one can make oneself happy thinking one has. And if one has money, may be one can make oneself happy by thinking one hasn't." He blinked at me, and then added, by way of solving all life's mysteries: "If one—puts too much store by these things."

I could find no remark to complement the postman's sententious conclusions, and, dismissing me with a nod, he mounted his bicycle and rode off up the hill.

Ned Picklekin was a stolid chunk of a young man, fair, blue-eyed, with his skin beaten to a uniform tint of warm red by the sun and wind. For he was the postman at the village of Ashalton. Except for two hours in the little sorting-office, he spent the whole day on his bicycle, invariably accompanied by his Irish terrier, Toffee. Toffee was as well known on the countryside as Ned himself. He took the business of delivering letters as seriously as his master. He trotted behind the bicycle with his tongue out, and waited panting outside the gates of gardens while the important government business was transacted. He never barked, and had no time for fighting common, unofficial dogs. When the letters were delivered, his master would return to his bicycle, and say: "Coom ahn, boy!" and Toffee would immediately jump up, and fall into line. They were great companions.

Ned lived with his mother, and also he walked out with a young lady. Her name was Ettie Skinner, and she was one of the three daughters of old Charlie Skinner, the corn-merchant. Charlie Skinner had a little establishment in the station-yard. He was a widower, and he and his three daughters lived in a cottage in Neap's Lane. It was very seldom necessary to deliver letters at the Skinners' cottage, but every morning Ned had to pass up Neap's Lane, and so, when he arrived at the cottage, he dismounted, and rang his bicycle bell. The signal was understood by Ettie, who immediately ran out to the gate, and a conversation somewhat on this pattern usually took place:

"Hulloa!"

"Hulloa!"

"All right?"

"Ay."

"Busy?"

"Ay. Mendin' some old cla'es."

"Oo-ay!"

"Looks like mebbe a shower."

"Mebbe."

"Coming' along to-night?"

"Ay, if it doan't rain."

"Well, so long!"

"So long, N'ed."

In the evenings the conversation followed a very similar course. They waddled along the lanes side by side, and occasionally gave each other a punch. Ned smoked his pipe all the time, and Toffee was an unembarrassed cicerone. He was a little jealous of this unnecessary female, but he behaved with a resigned acquiescence. His master could do no wrong. His master was a god, a being apart from all others.

It cannot be said that Ned was a romantic lover. He was solemn, direct, imperturbable. He was a Saxon of Saxons, matter-of-fact, incorruptible, unimaginative, strong-willed, conscientious, not very ambitious, and suspicious of the unusual and the unknown. When the war broke out, he said: "Ay, but this is a bad business!"

And thon he thought about it for a month. At the end of that time he made up his mind to join. He rode up Neap's Lane one morning and rang his bell. When Ettie appeared the usual conversation underwent a slight variant:

"Hulloa!"

"Hulloa!"

"All right?"

"Ay."

"Doin' much?"

"Oo—mendin' pa's night-gown."

"Oh! I be goin' to jine up."

"Oo-oh! Be'ee?"

"Ay."

"When be goin'?"

"Monday with Dick Thursby and Len Cotton. An' I think young Walters, and Bibbie Short mebbe."

"Oh, I say!"

"Ay. Comin' along to-night?"

"Av, if it doan't rain."

"Well, see you then."

"So long, Ned."

On the following Monday Ned said good-by to his mother, and sweetheart, and to Toffee, and he and the other four boys walked over to the recruiting office at Carchester. They were drafted into the same unit, and sent lip to Yorkshire to train.

(Yorkshire being one hundred and fifty miles away was presumably the most convenient and suitable spot.)

They spent five months there, and then Len Cotton was transferred to the Machine Gun Corps, and the other four were placed in an infantry regiment and sent out to India. They did not get an opportunity of returning to Ashalton, but the night before he left Ned wrote to his mother:

"Dear Mother, I think we are off to-morrow. They don't tell us where we are going but they seem to think it's India because of the Eastern kit served out and so on. Everything all right, the grub is fine. Young Walters has gone sick with a bile on his neck. Hope you are all right. See Toffee dont get into Mr. Mears yard for this is about the time he puts down that pison for the rats. Everything O. K. Love from Ned."

He wrote a very similar letter to Ettie, only leaving out the instructions about Toffee and adding "dont get overdoing it now the warm weathers on."

They touched at Gibraltar, Malta, Alexandria and Aden. At all these places he merely sent the cryptic postcard. He did not write a letter again until he had been three weeks up in the hills in India. As a matter of fact it had been a terribly rough passage nearly all the way, especially in the Mediterranean, and nearly all the boys had been sea-sick most of the time. Ned had been specially bad and in the Red Sea had developed a slight fever. In India he had been sent to a rest-camp up in the hills. He wrote:

"Dear mother, everything all right. The grub is fine. I went a bit sick coming out but nothing. Quite O. K. now. This is a funny place. The people would make you laugh to look at. We beat the 2nd Royal Scots by two goals to one. I wasn't playing but Binnie played a fine game at half back. He stopped their center forward, an old league player, time and again. Hope you are keeping all right. Does Henry Thatcham take Toffee out regler. Everything serene. Love from Ned."

In this letter the words "2nd Royal Scots" were deleted by the censor.

India at that time was apparently a kind of training-ground for young recruits. There were a few recalcitrant hill-tribes upon whom to practice the latest developments of military science, and Ned was mixed up in one or two of these little scraps' He proved himself a good soldier, doing precisely what he was told and being impervious to danger. They were five months in India, and then the regiment was suddenly drafted back to Egypt. Big things were afoot. No one knew what was going to happen. They spent ten days in a camp near Alexandria. They were then detailed for work in connection with the protection of the banks of the Canal, and Ned was stationed near the famous pyramid of Gizeh. He wrote to his mother:

"Dear mother, everything all right. Pretty quiet so far. This is a funny place. Young Walters has gone sick again. We had the regimental sports Thursday. Me and Bert Carter won the three-legged race.

 The grub is fine and we get dates and figs for nuts. Hope your cold is all right by now. Thanks for the parcel which I got on the 27th. Everything all right. Glad to hear about Mrs. Parsons having the twins and that. Glad to hear Toffee all right and so with love your loving son Ned."

They had not been at Gizeh for more than a week before they were sent back to Alexandria and placed on a transport. In fifteen days after touching at Imbros, Ned and his companions found themselves on Gallipoli peninsula. Heavy fighting was in progress. They were rushed up to the front line. For two days and nights they were in action and their numbers were reduced to one-third of their original size. For thirty hours they were without water and were being shelled by gas, harried by flame-throwers, blasted by shrapnel and high-explosive. At the end of that time they crawled back to the beach at night through prickly bramble which poisoned them and set up septic wounds if it scratched them. They lay there dormant for two days, but still under shell-fire, and then were hurriedly reformed into a new regiment, and sent to another part of the line. This went on continuously for three weeks, and then a terrible storm and flood occurred. Hundreds of men—some alive and some partly alive—were drowned in the ravines. Ned and his company lost all their kit, and slept in water for three nights running. At the end of four weeks he obtained five days' rest at the base. He wrote to Ettie:

"Dear Ettie, A long time since I had a letter from you. Hope all right. Everything all right so far. We had a bad storm but the weather now keeps fine. Had a fine bath this morning. There is a man in our company would make you laugh. He is an Irish-Canadian. He plays the penny whissle fine and sings a bit too. Sorry to say young Walters died. He got enteric and phewmonnia and so on. I expect his people will have heard all right. How is old Mrs. Walters? Dick Thursby got a packet too and Mrs. Quinby's boy I forget his name. How are them white rabbits of yours. I met a feller as used to take the milk round for Mr. Brand up at Bodes farm. Funny wasn't it. Well nothing more now. I hope this finds you as it leaves me your affectionate Ned."

Ned was three months on Gallipoli peninsula, but he left before the evacuation. During the whole of that time he was never not under shell-fire. He took part in seven attacks. On one occasion he went over the top with twelve hundred others, of whom only one hundred and seven returned. Once he was knocked unconscious by a mine explosion which killed sixty-seven men. At the end of that period he was shot through the back by a sniper. He was put in a dressing-station, and a gentleman in a white overall came and stuck a needle into his chest and left him there in a state of nudity for twelve hours. Work at the field hospitals was very congested just then. He became a bit delirious and was eventually put on a hospital ship with a little tag tied to him. After some vague and restless period he found himself again at Imbros and in a very comfortable hospital. He stayed there six weeks and his wound proved to be slight. The bone was only grazed. He wrote to his mother:

"Dear mother, Everything all right. I had a scratch but nothing. I hope you enjoyed the flower show. How funny meetings Mrs. Perks. We have a fine time here. The grub is fine. Sorry to say Binnie Short went under. He got gassed one night when he hadnt his mask on. The weather is mild and pleasant. Glad to hear Henry takes Toffee out all right. Have you heard from Ettie for some time. We had a fine concert on Friday. A chap played the flute lovely. Hope you are now all right again. Your loving son Ked."

In bed in the hospital at Imbros a bright idea occurred to Ned. He made his will. Such an idea would never have occurred to him had it not been forced upon him by the unusual experiences of the past year. He suddenly realized that of all the boys who had left the village with him only Len Cotton, as far as he knew, remained. So one night he took a blunt-pointed pencil, and laboriously wrote on the space for the will at the end of his pay-book:

"I leave everything I've got to my mother Anne Picklekin, including Toffee. I hope Henry Thatcham will continue to look after Toffee except the silver bowl which I won at the rabbit show at Oppleford. This I leave to Ettie Skinner as a memorial of me."

One day Ned enjoyed a great excitement. He was under discharge from the hospital, and a rumor got round that he and some others were to be sent back to England. They hung about the island for three days, and were then packed into an Italian fruit-steamer—which had been converted into a transport. It was very overcrowded and the weather was hot. They sailed one night and reached another island before dawn. They spent three weeks doing this. They only sailed at night, for the seas about there were reported to be infested with submarines. Every morning they put in at some island in the Greek Archipelago, or at some port on the mainland. At one place there was a terrible epidemic of illness, owing to some Greek gentlemen having sold the men some doped wine. Fifteen of them died. Ned escaped from this as he had not had any of the wine. He was practically a teetotaler except for an occasional glass of beer. But he was far from happy on that voyage. The seas were rough and the transport ought to have been broken up years ago, and this didn't seem to be the right route for England.

At length they reached a large port called Salonika. They never went into the town, but were sent straight out to a camp in the hills ten miles away. The country was very wild and rugged, and there was great difficulty with water. Everything was polluted and malarial. There was very little fighting apparently, but plenty of sickness. He found himself in a Scottish regiment. At least, it was called Scottish, but the men came from all parts of the world, from Bow Street to Hong- Kong.

There was to be no Blighty after all, but still—there it was! He continued to drill, and march, and clean his rifle and play the mouth-organ and football.

And then one morning he received a letter from his mother, which had followed him from Imbros. It ran as follows:

"My dear Ned, How are you, dear? I hope you keep all right. My corf is now pretty middlin otherwise nothin to complain of. Now dear I have to tell you something which grieves me dear. Im afraid its no good keepin it from you ony longer dear. Ettie is uialkin out ivith another feller. A feller from the air station called Alf Mullet. I taxed her with it and she says yes it is so dear. Now dear you mustnt take on about this. I told her off I says it was a disgraceful and you out there fightin for your country and that. And she says nothin excep yes there it was and she couldnt help it and her feelins had been changed you being away and that. Now dear you must put a good face on this and remember theres just as good fish in the sea as ever came out of it as they say dear. One of Mr. Bean's rabits died Sunday they think it overeating you never know with rabits. Keep your feet warm dear I hope you got them socks I sent. Lizzie was at chapel Sunday she had on her green lawn looked very nice I thought but I wish she wouldn't get them spots on her face perhaps its only the time of year. Toffee is all right he had a fight with a hairdale Thursday Henry-says got one of his eres bitten but nothin serous. So now dear I must close as Mrs. Minchin wants me to go and take tea with her has Florrie has gone to the school treat at Furley. And so dear with love your lovin Mother."

When he had finished reading this letter he uttered an exclamation, and a cockney friend sitting on the ground by his side remarked:

"What's the matter, mate?"

Ned took a packet of cigarettes out of his pocket and lighted one. Then he said:

"My girl's jilted me."

The cockney laughed and said:

"Gawd! is that all? I thought it was somthin' serious!"

He was cleaning his rifle with an oil rag, and he continued:

"Don't you worry, mate. Women are like those blinkin' little Greek islands, places to call at but not to stay. What was she like?"

"Oo—all right."

"Pretty?"

"Ay-middlin'."

"'As she got another feller?"

"Ay."

"Oh, well, it's all in the gime. If you will go gallivanting about these foreign parts enjoy' yerself, what d'yer expect? What time's kick off this afternoon?"

"Two o'clock."

"Reckon we're goin' to win?"

"I doan't know. 'Pends upon whether McFarlane turns out."

"Yus, 'e's a wonderful player. Keeps the team together like."

"Ay."

"Are you playin'?"

"Ay. I'm playin' right half."

"Are yer? Well, you'll 'ave yer 'ands full. You'll 'ave to tackle Curly Snider."

"Ay."

Ned's team won the match that afternoon, and he wrote to his mother afterwards:

"Dear mother, We just had a great game against 15 Royal South Hants. McFarlane played center half and he was in great form. We led 2-0 at half time and they scored one at the beginnin of the second half but Davis got throu towards the end and we beat them by 3-1. I was playin quite a good game I think but McFarlane is a real first class. I got your letter all right. I was sorry about Ettie but of course she knows what she wants I spose. You dont say what Toffee did to the other dog. You might tell Henry to let me have a line about this. Fancy Liz being at chapel. I almos forget what shes like.

Everything is all right. The grub is fine. This is a funny place all rocks and planes. The Greeks are a stinkin lot for the most part so now must close with love, Ned."

Having completed this letter, Ned got out his pay-book and revised his will. Ettie Skinner was now deleted, and the silver bowl won at the rabbit-show at Oppleford was bequeathed to Henry Thatcham in consideration of his services in taking Toffee out for runs.

They spent a long and tedious eight months on the plains of Macedonia, dodging malaria and bullets, cracking vermin in their shirts, playing football, ragging, quarreling, drilling, maneuvering and, most demoralizing of all, hanging about. And then a joyous day dawned. This hybrid Scottish regiment was ordered home! They left Salonika in a French liner and ten days later arrived at Malta. But in the mean-time the gods had been busy. The wireless operators had been flashing their mysterious signals all over the Mediterranean and the Atlantic. At Malta the order was countermanded. They remained there long enough to coal, but the men were not even given shore leave. The next day they turned eastwards again and made for Alexandria.

The cockney was furious. He had the real genius of the grouser, with the added venom of the man who in the year of grace had lived by his wits and now found his wits enclosed in an iron cylinder. It was a disgusting anti-climax.

"When I left that filthy 'ale," he exclaimed, "I swore to God I'd try and never remember it again. And now I'm darned if we ain't gain' back there. As if once ain't enough in a man's lifetime! It's like the blooming cat with the blankety mouse!"

"Eh, well, mon," interjected a Scotsman, "there's ane thing. They canna keel ye no but once."

"It ain't the killing I mind. It's the blooming mucking about. What d'yer say, Pickles?"

"Ah, well ... there it is," said Ned sententiously.

There was considerable "mucking about" in Egypt, and then they started off on a long trek through the desert, marching on barbed-wire mesh that had been laid down by the engineers. There was occasional skirmishing, sniping, fleas, delay, and general discomfort. One day, in Southern Palestine, Ned was out with a patrol party just before sun-down. They were trekking across the sand between two oases when two shots rang out. Five of the party fell. The rest were exposed in the open to foes firing from concealment on two sides. The position was hopeless. They threw up their hands. Two more shots rang out and the cockney next to Ned fell forward with a bullet through his throat. Then dark figures came across the sands towards them. There were only three left, Ned, a Scotsman, and a boy who had been a clerk in a drapery store at Lewisham before the war. He said:

"Well, are they going to kill us?"

"No," said the Scotsman. "Onyway, keep your hands weel up and pray to God."

A tall man advanced, and to their relief beckoned them to follow. They fell into single file.

"These are no Tur-r-ks at all," whispered the Scotsman. "They're some nomadic Arab tribe."
The Scotsman had attended evening continuation classes at Peebles, and was rather fond of the word "nomadic."

They were led to one of the oases, and instructed to sit down. The Arabs sat round them, armed with rifles. They remained there till late at night, when another party arrived, and a rope was produced. They were handcuffed and braced together, and then by gesticulation told to march.

They trailed across the sand for three hours and a half. There was no moon, but the night was tolerably clear. At length they came to another oasis, and were bidden to halt. They sat on the sand for twenty minutes, and one of the Arabs gave them some water. Then a whistle blew, and they were kicked and told to follow. The party wended its way through a grove of cedar trees. It was pitch dark. At last they came to a halt by a large hut. There was much coming and going. When they entered the hut, in charge of their guard, they were blinded by a strong light. The hut was comfortably furnished and lighted by electric light. At a table sat a stout, pale-faced man, with a dark mustache—obviously a German. By his side stood a tall German orderly. The German official looked tired and bored. He glanced at the prisoners and drew some papers towards him.

"Come and stand here in front of my desk," he said in English.

They advanced, and he looked at each one carefully. Then he yawned, dipped his pen in the ink, tried it on a sheet of paper, swore, and inserted a fresh nib.

"Now, you," he said, addressing the Scotsman, when he had completed these operations. "Name, age, profession, regiment. Smartly."

He obtained all these particulars from each man. Then he got up and came round the table, and looking right into the eyes of the clerk from Lewisham, he said:

"We know, of course, in which direction your brigade is advancing, but from which direction is the brigade commanded by Major-General Forbes Fittleworth advancing?"

The three of them all knew this, for it was common gossip of the march. But the clerk from Lewisham said:

"I don't know."

The German turned from him to the Scotsman and repeated the question. "I don't know," answered the Scotsman.

"From which direction is the brigade commanded by Major-General Forbes Fittleworth advancing?" he said to Ned. "Naw! I doan't know," replied Ned.

And then a horrible episode occurred. The German suddenly whipped out a revolver and shot the clerk from Lewisham through the body twice. He gave a faint cry and crumpled forward. Without taking the slightest notice of this horror, the German turned deliberately and held the revolver pointed at Ned's face. In a perfectly unimpassioned, toneless voice he repeated:

"From which direction is the brigade commanded by Major-General Forbes Fittleworth advancing?" In the silence which followed, the only sound seemed to be the drone of some machine, probably from the electric-light plant. The face of Ned was mildly surprised but quite impassive. He answered without a moment's hesitation:

"Naw! I doan't know."

There was a terrible moment in which the click of the revolver could almost be heard. It seemed to hover in front of his face for an unconscionable time, then suddenly the German lowered it with a curse, and leaning forward, he struck Ned on the side of his face with the flat of his hand. He treated the Scotsman in the same way, causing his nose to bleed. Both of the men remained quite impassive. Then he walked back to his seat, and said calmly:

"Unless you can refresh your memories within the next two hours you will share the fate of—that swine. You will now go out to the plantation at the back and dig your graves. Dig three graves."

He spoke sharply in Arabic to the guards, and they were led out. They were handed a spade each, two Arabs held torches for them to work by, and four others hovered in a circle twelve paces away. The soil was light sand, and digging was fairly easy. Each man dug his own grave making it about four feet deep. When it came to the third grave the Scotsman whispered:

"Dig deep, mon."

"Deeper than others?"

"Ay, deep enough to make a wee trench."

"I see."

They made it very deep, working together and whispering. When it was practically completed, apparently a sudden quarrel arose between the men. They swore at each other, and the Scotsman sprang out of the trench and gripped Ned by the throat. A fearful struggle began to take place on the edge of the grave. The guard ran up and tried to separate them. And then, during the brief confusion there was a sudden dramatic development. Simultaneously they snatched their spades. Both the men with the torches were knocked senseless, and one of them fell into the third grave.

The torches were stamped out and a rifle went off. It was fired by a guard near the hut, and the bullet struck another Arab who was trying to use his bayonet. Ned brought a fourth man down with his spade and seized his rifle, and the Scotsman snatched the rifle of the man who had been shot, and they both leapt back into their purposely prepared trench.

"We shallna be able to hold this long, but we'll give them a run for their money," said the Scotsman.

The body of one Arab was lying on the brink of their trench and the other in the trench itself. Fortunately they both had bandoliers, which Ned and his companion instantly removed.

"You face east and I'll take west," said the Scotsman, his eyes glittering in the dim light. "I'm going to try and scare that Boche devil."

He peppered away at the hut, putting bullets through every window and smashing the telephone connection, which was a fine target at the top of a post against the sky. Bullets pinged over their heads from all directions, but there was little chance of them being rushed while their ammunition held out. However, it became necessary to look ahead. It was the Scotsman'-s idea in digging the graves to plan them in zig-zag formation. The end of the furthest one was barely ten paces from a clump of aloes. He now got busy with his spade whilst Ned kept guard in both directions, occasionally firing at the hut and then in the opposite direction into the darkness. In half-an-hour the Scotsman had made a shallow connection between the three graves, leaving just enough room to crawl through. They then in turn donned the turbans of the two fallen Arabs, who were otherwise dressed in a kind of semi-European uniform.

They ended up with a tremendous fusillade against the hut, riddling it with bullets; then they crept to the end of the furthest grave, and leaving their rifles, they made a sudden dash across the open space to the group of aloes, bending low and limping like wounded Arabs.

They reached them in safety, but there were many open spaces to cover yet. As they emerged from the trees Ned stumbled on a dark figure. He kicked it and ran. They both ran zig-zag fashion, and tore off their turbans as they raced along. They covered nearly a hundred yards, and then bullets began to search them out again. They must have gone nearly a mile before the Scotsman gave a sudden slight groan.

'I'm hit," he said.

He stumbled into a clump of bushes, and fell down.

"Is it bad?" asked Ned.

"Eh, laddie, I'm doon," he said quietly. He put his hand to his side. He had been shot through the lungs. Ned stayed with him all night, and they were undisturbed. Just before dawn the Scotsman said:

"Eh, mon, but yon was a bonny fight," and he turned on his back and died. Ned made a rough grave with his hands, and buried his companion. He took his identification-disc and his pocket-book and small valuables, with the idea of returning them to his kin if he should get through himself. He also took his water flask, which still fortunately contained a little water. He lay concealed all day, and at night he boldly donned his turban, issued forth and struck a caravan-trail. He continued this for four days and nights hiding in the day-time and walking at night. He lived on figs and dates, and one night he raided a village and caught a fowl, which also nearly cost him his life.

On the fourth night his water gave out, and he was becoming light-headed. He stumbled on into the darkness. He was a desperate man. All the chances were against him, and he felt unmoved and fatalistic. He drew his clasp-knife and gripped it tightly in his right hand. He was hardly conscious of what he was doing, and where he was going. The moon was up, and after some hours he suddenly beheld a small oblong hut. He got it into his head that this was the hut where his German persecutor was. He crept stealthily towards it. "I'll kill that swine," he muttered.

He was within less than a hundred yards of the hut, when a voice called out: "'Alt! Who goes there?"

"It's me," he said. "Doan't thee get in my way. I want to kill him. I'm going to kill him. I'm going to, I tell you. I'm going to stab him through his black heart."

"What the hell!"

The sentry was not called upon to use his rifle, for the turbaned figure fell forward in a swoon. Three weeks later Ned wrote to his mother from Bethlehem (where Christ was born), and this is what he said:

"Dear mother, Everything going on all right. I got three parcels here altogether as I had been away copped by some black devils an unfriendly tribe. I got back all right though. The ointment you sent me was fine and so was them rock cakes. What a funny thing about Belle getting lost at the picnick. We got an awful soaking from the Mid-Lanes Fusiliers on Saturday. They had two league cracks playing one a wonderful center forward. He scored three goals. They beat us by 7-0. The weather is hot but quite pleasant at night. We have an old sergeant who was born in America does wonderful tricks with string and knots and so on. He tells some very tall yarns. You have to take them with a pinch of salt. Were getting fine grub here pretty quiet so far. Hope Henry remembers to wash Toffee with that stuff every week or so. Sony to hear Len Cotton killed. Is his sister still walking out with that feller at Aynliam. I never think he was much class for her getting good money though. Hope you have not had any more trouble with the boiler. That was a good price to get for that old buck rabbit. Well there's nothing more just now and so with love your loving son, Ned."

Ned went through the Palestine campaign and was slightly wounded in the thigh. After spending some time in hospital he was sent to the coast and put on duty looking after Turkish prisoners. He remained there six months and was then shipped to Italy. On the way the transport was torpedoed. He was one of a painty of fifty-seven picked up by French destroyers. He had been for over an hour in the water in his lifebelt. He was landed in Corsica and there he developed pneumonia. He only wrote his mother one short note about this:

"Dear mother, Have been a bit dicky owing to falling in the water and getting wet. But going on all right. Nurses very kind and one of the doctors rowed for Cambridge against Oxford. I forget the year but Cambridge won by two and a half lengths. We have very nice flowers in the ward. Well not much to write about and so with love your loving son, Ned."

Ned was fit again in a few weeks and he was sent up to the Italian front. He took part in several engagements and was transferred to the French front during the last months of the war. He was in the great retreat in March 1918 and in the advance in July. After the armistice he was with the army of occupation on the banks of the Rhine. His mother wrote to him there:

"My dear Ned, Am glad that this fighting is now all over dear. How relieved you must be. Mr. Filter was in Sunday. He thinks there will be no difficulty about you gettin your job back when you come back dear. Miss Siffkins as been deliverin but as Mr. Filter says its not likely a girl is going to be able to deliver letters not like a man can and that dear. So now you will be comin home soon dear. That will be nice. We had a pleesant afternoon at the Church needlewomens gild. Miss Barbary Banstock sang very pleesantly abide with me and the vicar told a very amusing story about a little girl and a prince and she didn't know he was a prince and talked to him just as though he was a man it was very amusin dear. I hear Ettie is goin to get married next month they wont get me to the weddin was it ever so I call it disgraceful and I have said so. Maud Bean is expectin in April that makes her forth in three years. Mr. Bean has lost three more rabbits they say its rats this time. The potatoes are a poor lot this time but the runners and cabbidge promiss well. So now dear I will close. Hoppin to have your back dear soon, your loving mother."

It was, however, the autumn before Ned was demobilized. One day in early October he came swinging up the village street carrying a white kit-bag slung across his left shoulder. He looked more bronzed and perhaps a little thinner, but otherwise little altered by his five years of war experiences. The village of Ashalton was quite unaltered, but he observed several strange faces; he only met two acquaintances on the way to his mother's cottage, and they both said:

"Hullo, Ned! Ye're home agen then!" In each case he replied:

"Ay," and grinned, and walked on.

He entered his mother's cottage, and she was expecting him. The lamp was lighted and a grand tea spread. There was fresh boiled beetroot, tinned salmon, salad, cake, and a large treacle tart. She embraced him and said:

"Well, Ned! Ye're back then."

He replied, "Ay."

"Ye're lookin fine," she said. "What a fine suit they've given ye!"

"Ay," he replied.

"I expect you want yer tea?"

"Ay."

He had dropped his kit-bag, and he moved luxuriously round the little parlor, looking at all the familiar objects... Then he sat down, and his mother brought the large brown tea-pot from the hob and they had a cozy tea. She told him all the very latest news of the village, and all the gossip of the countryside, and Ned grinned and listened. He said nothing at all. The tea had progressed to the point when Ned's mouth was full of treacle tart when his mother suddenly stopped, and said:

"Oh, dear, I'm afraid I have somethin' distressin' to tell ye, dear."

"O-oh? what's that?"

"Poor Toffee was killed."

"What!"

Ned stopped suddenly in the mastication of the treacle tart. His eyes bulged and his cheeks became very red. He stared at his mother wildly, and repeated.

"What's that? What's that ye say, mother?"

"Poor Toffee, my dear. It happened right at the cross-roads. Henry was takin' him out. It seems he ran round in front of a steam-roller, and a motor came round the corner sudden. Henry called out, but too late. Went right over his back. Poor Henry was quite upset. He brought him home. What's the matter, dear?"

Ned had pushed his chair back and he stood up. He stared at his mother like a man who has seen horror for the first time.

"Where is he—where was—" he stammered.

"We buried 'im, dear, under the little mound beyond the rabbit hutches." Ned staggered across the room like a drunken man, and repeated dismally: "The little mound beyond the rabbit hutches!" He lifted the latch, and groped his way into the garden. His mother followed him. He went along the mud path, past the untenanted hutches covered with tarpaulin. Some tall sunflowers stared at him insolently. A fine rain was beginning to fall. In the dim light he could just see the little mound—signifying the spot where Toffee was buried. He stood there bareheaded, gazing at the spot. His mother did not like to speak. She tiptoed back to the door. But after a time she called out:

"Ned! ... Ned!"

He did not seem to hear, and she waited patiently. At the end of several minutes she called again: "Ned! ... Ned dear, come and finish your tea." He replied quite quietly:

"All right, mother."

But he kept his face averted, for he did not want his mother to see the tears which were streaming down his cheeks.

Stacy Aumonier was born at Hampstead Road near Regent's Park, London on 31st March 1877.

He came from a family with a strong and sustained tradition in the visual arts; sculptors and painters.

In 1890 the teenage Aumonier attended Cranleigh School in Surrey. Although he would later write critically about English public schools (with articles for the London Evening Standard and New York Times) in how they tried to impose conformity on students, records indicate that he integrated well into Cranleigh. Aumonier was a passionate cricket player, belonged to the Literary and Debating Society, and, in his final year, became a prefect.

On leaving school it seemed the family tradition of the visual arts would be his career path. In particular his early talents were that of a landscape painter. He exhibited paintings at the Royal Academy in 1902 and 1903, and 1908. An exhibition of his work would later be held at the Goupil Gallery in London in 1911.

In 1907 he married the international concert pianist, Gertrude Peppercorn, at West Horsley in Surrey. She herself was the daughter of a landscape painter (Arthur Douglas Peppercorn, occasionally cited as 'the English Corot'.) A son, Timothy, was born in 1921.

A year after his marriage, Aumonier began a brief career in a second branch of the arts at which he enjoyed outstanding success—as a stage performer writing and performing his own sketches.

The Observer newspaper commented that "...the stage lost in him a real and rare genius, he could walk out alone before any audience, from the simplest to the most sophisticated, and make it laugh or cry at will."

In 1915, Aumonier published a short story 'The Friends' which was well received (and voted one of the best short stories of 1915 by the Boston Magazine, Transcript).

Despite his age being 40 in 1917 he was called up for service in World War I. He began as a private in the Army Pay Corps, and then transferred as a draughtsman in the Ministry of National Service.

By now he had four books published—two novels and two books of short stories—and his occupation is recorded with the Army Medical Board as 'author.'

In the mid-1920s, Aumonier received the shattering diagnosis that he had contracted tuberculosis. In the last few years of his life, he would spend long spells in various sanatoria, some better than others. In a letter to his friend, Rebecca West, written shortly before his death, he described the debilitating conditions in a sanatorium in Norfolk during the winter of 1927, where the dampness was so severe that a newspaper left beside the bed would feel "sodden to the touch in the morning."

Shortly before his death, Stacy Aumonier sought treatment in Switzerland, but died of the disease in Clinique La Prairie at Clarens beside Lake Geneva on 21st December 1928. He was 55.

Whilst Aumonier's works are now slowly coming back into circulation at the time of his death his works were extremely popular and his loss was a profound tragedy for literary society.

The chief fiction critic of The Observer, Gerald Gould wrote: "His gifts were almost fantastically various; they embraced all the arts; but it was the charm and generosity of his personality which made him—what he unquestionably was—one of the most popular men of his generation." It went on: "The things he wrote will be remembered when the company of his friends (no man had more friends, or more devoted and admiring) are with him in the grave; but just now, to those who knew him, the thing most vividly present is the charm and wisdom of the man they knew."

Of his general appearance and manner Gerald Cumberland gives us this interesting set of observations: "A distinguished man, this—distinguished both in mind and appearance. Self-conscious. Perhaps. Why not? His hair is worn a trifle long, and it is arranged so that his fine forehead, broad and high, may be fully revealed. Round his neck is a very high collar and a modern stock. When in repose, his face has a look of shy eagerness; his quick eyes glance here and there gathering a thousand impressions to be stored up in his brain. It is the face of a man extremely sensitive to external stimulus; one feels that his brain works not only rapidly, but with great accuracy. And at heart, he takes himself and his work seriously, though he likes on occasion to pretend that he is only a philanderer."

In literary terms Aumonier was amongst the best short story writers these shores have produced.

The Nobel Prize winning author John Galsworthy called him "A real master of the short story. The first essential in a short-story writer is the power of interesting sentence by sentence. Aumonier had this power in prime degree. You do not have to 'get into' his stories. He is especially notable for investing his figures with the breadth of life within a few sentences." Galsworthy asserted that Aumonier "is never heavy, never boring, never really trivial; interested himself, he keeps us interested. At the back of his tales, there is belief in life and a philosophy of life, and of how many short story writers can that be said? ...He follows no fashion and no school. He is always himself. And can't he write? Ah! Far better than far more pretentious writers. Nothing escapes his eye, but he describes without affectation or redundancy, and you sense in him a feeling for beauty that is never obtruded. He gets values right, and that is to say nearly everything. The easeful fidelity of his style has militated against his reputation in these somewhat posturing times. But his shade may rest in peace, for in this volume, at least he will outlive nearly all the writers of his day." In summing his up Galsworthy suggested that, through his stories, he would "outlive all the writers of his day."

James Hilton (author of Goodbye, Mr Chips and Lost Horizon) said "I think his very best works ought to be included in any anthology of the best short stories ever written." He cited 'The Octave of Jealously' as his favourite short story for the March 1939 edition of Good Housekeeping saying it was a "bitterly brilliant tale."

Rebecca West said of his writing in 1922 that his ability to blend reality with the imaginary was "the envy of all artists."

Stacy Aumonier – A Concise Bibliography

More than 87 short stories in more than 25 magazines, and in 6 volumes published during Aumonier's lifetime.

Among more than 20 other magazines, his work appeared in Argosy Magazine, John O' London's Weekly, The Strand Magazine and The Saturday Evening Post, as well as being anthologized, and adapted for film and television.

Short Story Collections

The Golden Windmill & Other Stories (1921)
The Friends & Other Stories (1917)
Miss Bracegirdle & Other Stories (1923)

Novels

Olga Bardel (1916)
Three Bars Interval (1917)
Just Outside (1917)
The Querrils (1919)
One After Another (1920)
Heartbeat (1922)

Other Works

A volume of 14 Character Studies: Odd Fish (1923)

A volume of 15 Essays: Essays of Today and Yesterday (1926)